THE HILL

ALI BRYAN

dottir
press

NEW YORK

Published in 2021 by Dottir Press
33 Fifth Avenue
New York, NY 10003

Dottirpress.com

FIRST EDITION
First printing December 2020

Cover illustration by Eglė Plytnikaitė
Production and design by Frances Ross

Trade distribution by Consortium Book Sales and Distribution,
www.cbsd.com.

Library of Congress Cataloging-in-Publication Data is available for this title.
ISBN 978-1948-340-328 (pbk)
ISBN 978-1948-340-342 (ebook)
Library of Congress Control Number: 2020952288

Manufactured in the USA by McNaughton & Gunn.

For my girls, Pippa and Odessa,
who live wholly, wildly, brightly, boldly.

And to the next generation of girls: go get it.

CHAPTER 1

Section 5.8 – All girls over the age of fifteen must leave the Hill.

I STAND ON the Hill's summit alone, like the spire atop a watchtower. Up here, the wind is violent. It rolls off the ocean 753 steps below and then charges up, stinging the cheeks and whipping the braids of girls as it climbs. If you're afraid of heights, don't look down. Don't look up, either. You look up too quick, the sun will blind your eyes and freckle your face while the clouds yank you over the edge. And as much as you want them to soothe your wounds and cradle you like a baby, they'll let you drop. They'll even kiss you on the way down.

"Wren," Quinn hollers, "you're going to be late."

I glance at the sun, at the muted gold beams fanning the horizon, then look downhill. She's probably right. The Collectors have already abandoned the grassy southwest slope. All that remains are the makeshift stakes and ropes they've used to grid off a steep portion

5

of the Hill and a trio of sad seagulls drifting in circles they can't seem to escape.

"Wren," Quinn calls again, cupping her hands around her mouth. "You've got five minutes."

I grab my shovel, light as kindling, with its splintered handle and dull blade. I inherited it from a previous Collector, whose name is still carved into the shaft. *Pippa.* I lift the patch off my right eye and take a final, dizzying look down. Forty-one girls mobilize toward the giant Rock in the middle of the Hill. In a few minutes, a Departure Ceremony will release eleven of them.

I slip the patch back on and blink, adjusting my lashes. Am I blind in that eye? Partially. Probably would've been fully blind, if I hadn't started taking the patch off when no one was around, willing the muscles to perform. I should leave it off altogether, see whether I can restore my vision completely. But other than the threadbare clothes on my back, a square of replacement patch fabric, and a few strings of spare elastic, it's all I had when I arrived here and all I'll have when I leave. *Always wear your patch.*

"Wren!" Louder this time. Quinn's fists rest on her broad hips, her chest proud and lips pursed. An angry goddess. My best friend.

I've already begun the descent, skidding down the steep parts. The treads of my boots are worn and smooth as sea glass. I use the shovel for balance. "Coming," I shout.

She waits impatiently, hanging off her spear, which she's driven into the ground like a spike.

6

Loose rocks slide beneath my feet, and I nearly fall. "I'll just meet you down there."

Quinn throws her hands up, rips her spear from the ground, and stomps further downhill, toward the Departure Ceremony. Her black hair, tangled like a mass of seaweed, bounces with each step. Girls in her way clear a path.

I ditch my shovel on top of a heap of tools and poke my head through the Quarters' crude opening. It's less a door and more a ragged hole, girl-height and suitably wide. The entire shelter is built into the hillside and smells like spring and unwashed hair. Cozy. No one is inside, except for Ember.

"Come here, you." I slap my thigh, and she jumps up, pressing her paws into my ribcage, forcing me to take a step back. I inspect her face. "You're filthy." She wags her tail and turns in a circle as I pluck a twig from her fur. "Are you coming?" Her bark makes me flinch.

I twist my hair into a knot on top of my head, using sweat to smooth down the flyaways. It must be a thousand degrees, the kind of heat that bends your vision and burns your shoulders. "Let's go, then."

After the Departure Ceremony, the eleven girls will be gone. I am not one of them because I am fourteen years and 363 days old. The number of days is significant. Those two days keeping me fourteen are what separate me from the girls who go. It's simple. But there's another thing about those days—they make me the oldest one left behind, and that detail alone makes me the Head Girl.

CHAPTER 2

Section 4.6 – All babies arriving on the Hill must be received, named, and documented in the Record, including those who don't make the crossing from the Mainland. Each girl should be given an Assignment at the age of four, which they will maintain until their departure.

I FOLLOW QUINN'S path downward. Seven days, and *she* would have been the Head Girl. I balk at the thought; we'd have to rename the position to Dictator.

The island we live on is shaped like a sleeping girl, her knees tucked, spine curving north. The Hill is her left hip. Whoever conjured that image never had to share a bed with Quinn. But from here, it looks nothing like a girl. Just a massive expanse of land that continues indefinitely and rolls into forest—one that spans from west to north, which we can navigate blindfolded—and the other to the east, so dense and tightly packed that it's like walking through a hairbrush. Not that it matters. We're not allowed to go in it.

I stop midway to pick a flower. It's in full bloom, with drowsy white petals. I shorten the stem with my knife, which stains my fingers green, and I stick the blossom in my hair. Ember stops to sniff a dead bird. It's a tiny thing, its beak the size of a fingernail, feathers still young with fluff.

"Don't eat it," I caution. "We don't know how it died."

Ember cocks her head to the side and carries on.

I'm one of the last Collectors to reach the meeting point. The Smalls—those who are four years and younger—have already assembled in front of the Rock with their Mothers. They look like sparrows crowded at its base. The Rock is imposing, at least eight feet tall at its highest point, but climbable if you get a running start. While the front is pigeon-gray and rough as an elbow, the back is smooth and covered in the graffitied names of girls. And though many of those names belong to girls who've left the Hill, only Tora's name is scratched out.

Quinn tugs at my shirt and pats the ground. "Here."

I oblige and sit cross-legged beside her. Ember wedges herself between us with the finesse of a marmot.

Quinn surveys the top of my head. "What's with the flower?"

I shrug. "It made me feel optimistic."

"It looks kinda stupid," she says. "Besides, you should be nervous. In a few hours, this is all you." She sweeps her arm from one side of the Hill to the other.

"Thanks for the reminder." I jab her with my elbow.

"I'm kidding." She pokes the flower deeper in place behind my ear and brushes a strand of hair from my shoulder.

Ember rolls onto her side and stretches her neck, her

eyes blue as a vein. I rub her belly. *Where did she even come from?*

Quinn shifts to make room. "Dog's only been here for a few weeks and already she thinks she owns you."

I wink. "Does that make you jealous?"

A group of Foragers files in, their cattail sacks weighed down from the morning haul.

"I hope they have blackberries in one of those," Quinn mutters. "I'll die if I have to eat any more bog myrtle."

"I'd rather eat bog myrtle than crickets," I reply. "I swear I could hear them chirping inside my stomach last night."

Quinn chews on a piece of grass. "You should've had the soup."

Ember barks and we both jump. A Small sitting across from us plugs her ears, her hair a bird's nest.

I pull a map from my pocket, the paper yellowed and stained with fingerprints, and flatten it across my lap. MEETING POINT is written in fancy script next to a crude drawing of a rock.

"Why do you have that?" Quinn asks.

"Beck gave it to me."

"What for?"

"I don't know. A Head Girl thing, I guess. She just said I should have it."

"Useless, if you ask me."

"I didn't."

Quinn frowns.

"Sorry," I mumble. "I want to be prepared."

Quinn leans in, studies the map, and finger-reads

the legend. "Blah, blah, blah, *don't go anywhere below the knees.*" She points to the island's ankles and recites, "Limestone Pass. *Where one cannot walk barefoot.*"

Above the neck is also off-limits. There's no label indicating why; it's just completely black. Snuffed out, like her head was a flame. Beside it, someone wrote Tora's name with a question mark.

Quinn points to it. "There's no way she went that way."

"Why not?"

"The Manual said she was last seen down here." Quinn circles the island's shins. "Barefoot to boot. She probably bled to death on the limestone or got trapped in a crevice."

"But a Hunter said that's not true. You of all girls should believe that. She said Tora disappeared here, where the map turns black."

Quinn smirks. "You weren't even here."

I hate when she points that out. "And you were just a baby."

"Exactly. And I've been hearing about it ever since. It's the book my Mother used to teach me to read: *The Disappearance of Arrival # 97.* I think I've read it nine-ty-seven times. *'Late one night, Tora disappeared into the Eastside Forest with only a...*'"

"'*Sack and a slingshot,*' I know."

"See? Old news." She sighs, turning away. "Talk to me when you find a map of the Mainland. Staring at *that* is a waste of time."

But it's not. There's a mark I've never noticed before

11

on the island's blackened north corner. Nothing discernible, but definitely a symbol. An asterisk? A flag?

A single streaky cloud underlines the sun as a group of Hunters gathers behind us, bows and arrows strapped to their backs, a few with spears, like Quinn. I fold the map, and stuff it back in my pocket. The Suppliers, who prepare the meals and make things out of whatever we dig up, stack bags of food beside the Rock and file in beside the Mothers. The Collectors, to which I am assigned, are scattered about, comparing notes on the morning haul.

"Finally," Quinn says, as the eleven Departing Girls assemble in front of the rock in a curved line that's reminiscent of an eyelash. In front of them is Beck, our current Head Girl. Her face is blotchy with tears, and her shoulders slump inward. One of the Smalls scrambles to her feet, twig arms swinging, and attaches herself to Beck's leg. Beck tries to peel the Small's fingers off her thigh, gently at first and then forcefully. The Small's Mother, Harlow, sets down one of the other children she's caring for and ushers the escapee back to join the rest of the girls. The child thrashes on Harlow's lap, kicking her legs and flailing her arms. Harlow whispers something, and in seconds, the Small settles, sucking on her fist.

Quinn nudges my shoulder. "I'm so glad I wasn't assigned to be a Mother."

"Me too," I reply, though part of me wishes I had. Raising the Smalls is the most important of the Assignments. "I don't have that kind of patience."

Beck takes a meditative breath and starts the Departure Ceremony. I tune out when she starts reading from the Manual, with its never-ending lists and guidelines and rules and how-tos. How to harvest a deer. How to frame a wall. How to read. How to make fuel. How to extract a tooth, tie a knot, escape a rip current, program a boat. How to choke someone out—cold. How to, how to, how to.

I pick at a ruptured callus on my palm, recalling the first time I saw the brick-thick Manual, each page meticulously labeled, hole-punched, and hand-stamped with the word COLONY on the bottom-right corner. The same word is inked on the back of my neck, on the back of all the girls' necks. I run my finger along my hairline, feeling for it.

Quinn, unable to sit still, inspects the tip of her spear and polishes it with her spit. A page falls from the Manual, then another, their edges torn and filthy. Beck mumbles in frustration and stoops to gather the pieces. She struggles to fit the pages back in place, the book teetering in her hand. I remember asking my Mother why the Manual was so big, why it was so heavy, why there were so many pages. I'd just arrived, seasick and stunned, the only child in a boat brimming with babies, books, and supplies. *You ask too many questions*, she replied before showing me my assigned bed. Then she stopped to wipe my face and whispered, *The Manual is big because we have to learn how to do everything.*

"That's how we survive," Beck says, clearing her throat and continuing the ceremony. "For sixty . . ." she pauses to count her fingers. "Sixty-seven years, the Colony continues to be a place of safety, progress, and hope."

"It is the only way," Quinn whispers mockingly, in unison with Beck.

I stifle a smile. Ember licks my hand.

Beck gets to the part where the Departing Girls are told to give away their personal belongings. My Mother left me a pen during the last Ceremony, and it still hasn't run out of ink. The pens we find on the Hill usually only last a day—if that—before they run dry and are repurposed as stakes or hair accessories. Another time, a Supplier gifted me a knit hat that I wore until it unraveled.

Nova steps out of line. She's beautiful, with nearly translucent hair and clay-colored eyes. She kneels in front of me and says, "Open your hand." I stretch my fingers, and she presses a wad of yellow cloth into my palm. I spread it out on the ground. It's a T-shirt—a real one. What I wear now is something a Supplier constructed from scraps of fabric recovered from a previous dig. It's asymmetrical, longer on the left than the right, and there's a hole in the back where my shoulder blade pops through, as if it was designed to accommodate the growth of a wing.

Nova blows her hair off her forehead, her face flushed from the afternoon heat. "Try it on."

A portion of the shirt's neck is ripped, and there's a small stain on the side, but otherwise it's perfect. I kiss her on the cheek. "Where'd you find it?"

"I've been saving it for a while," she says. "It's you." She steps back in line, and Beck continues the Ceremony.

Quinn slumps beside me, empty-handed. I put my arm around her. "It's not personal," I console her. "You're one of the strongest girls out here. Everyone knows it. You already have everything you need."

She lifts her chin and shrugs. We both know she's more bothered by the kiss. "Some things *are* personal."

"Yes, like goodbyes." I watch Nova return to the line of Departing Girls.

Ember rests her head on Quinn's lap and whimpers. *How did she get here?* I imagine a shipwreck, or some valiant swim from who-knows-where.

"What kinds of Assignments do you think they'll get on the Mainland?" Quinn asks.

I shrug. "I assume more of the same if the Colony's going to continue to survive. Mother, Hunter, Supplier—"

Quinn interrupts, "—Forager, Collector; I get it. I was just hoping there might be more. Like, I don't know." She pauses to flick away an ant perusing her shin. "Like, Builder or Maker or Singer."

"You're a terrible singer." I laugh, rocking back on my tailbone. Ember wags her tail as if in agreement. "Besides, I'm sure the Colony hasn't survived this long because of Singers. '*Quick! There's an unidentified person approaching the North Gate—sing!*'"

Quinn smiles. "Well, I can hum."

"You can hum; I'll give you that. But you're the best hunter I know. One-shot Quinn." I mock-shoot an arrow, drawing my elbow back and squinting my good eye.

"The Colony's survived this long," she muses. "Maybe by the time we Depart, there'll be new Assignments."

"It's survived this long because no one knows about it. You know any Assignment, new or otherwise, will be designed to keep it that way." I stare at Beck. Written on the back of her hand are the GPS coordinates she'll use to get to the Mainland. She would've pulled them from section 3.6 of the Manual: TECHNOLOGY. It's only half a page, but it's the one section the Colony frequently updates. So many subsections, so many amendments.

Quinn leans into me. "At least they have GPS. In the beginning, they just had a compass and a map. Can you imagine what that would've been like at night? Pitch-black?"

In line, Nova shifts her weight from hip to hip and shakes her legs alternately, like she's anticipating the start of a race. The girl beside her, a Mother, frantically bites her thumbnail.

"Don't you wish we were going?" Quinn whispers, examining the tip of an arrow.

I don't immediately reply. Section 2 describes the Mainland as "overcrowded, hostile, and lawless." Chaos on every corner, whole sections in ruins, not enough food. Somewhere hidden on it is the Colony: a community restricted to and run by women. The only part of the Mainland that's thriving. Humanity's only hope. It's the whole reason we're here. She knows this. It's how the Manual starts.

"I like the Hill," I say at last. "It's private. And peaceful."

"But aren't you tired of all the training? The routine? The same thing every day? Wake up, eat, work, eat, work, eat, sleep, repeat. What good is learning all this stuff and 'developing skills' if we don't get to use them?"

"We use them every day," I argue. "We can dig and build and eat and drink. We have shelter. Weapons. I even have a three-legged chair."

"And crickets."

"Yes." I laugh. "An abundance of them."

Beck waves an arm. "Wren, get up here."

I stand nervously. Beck takes off the official Head Girl necklace she's worn for the last couple of years. It's a leather cord, knotted and frayed, strung with items girls dug up or left behind: a wishbone, a green gem, a few coins, and some shells and beads and bits. The necklace gets caught in Beck's hair, which is big and amazing, a black dandelion gone to seed, and drapes the thing around my neck. The enormity of what's happening suddenly strikes me like a switch to the back of the legs.

Beck takes my hand and raises my arm. I swallow hard, and everyone claps, except Quinn, who jams a pair of fingers in her mouth and whistles obnoxiously.

Beck squeezes my shoulders and turns back to the girls. "Let's wrap this up." She opens one of the cloth packs, removes a water bottle, and takes a swig. Water drips down her neck. "Say your goodbyes," she shouts.

The line of Departing Girls collapses in on the rows

of girls who will remain on the Hill. The Lead Supplier weaves through the chaos, distributing the remaining food packs to the Departing Girls. I try to see what they're being sent off with when Beck grabs my wrist and yanks me behind the rock. When we're out of sight, she pins me against it and grabs my face. I hold my breath.

"Listen to me."

I gulp.

"There have been sightings over the last few days."

"Sightings?"

"Of others." Her eyes are pleading, swollen ponds.

"Other . . . girls?"

I wait, but she doesn't elaborate, only stares, her expression grave, like there's something fast and horrific behind me that she knows I can't outrun.

"Just—just keep an eye out, Wren. Be vigilant. Assign more girls to defense at night." She points a finger at me. "And don't forget your head counts."

"But we need Mothers." My protest is quiet. "There's hardly enough as it is."

She pulls me away from the rock, my new shirt gathered in her fists. "Are you listening?" she hisses through clenched teeth.

I flinch, my mind racing. *What does she mean by sightings? How can she leave?*

"You can't leave."

Beck ignores me. "There won't be any more babies for at least a year." She looks around as if someone might be listening. "There's trouble on the Mainland."

"There's always trouble on the Mainland."

She lets go of my shirt, uncrumples a wad of paper from her sack, and holds it against the rock. "I found this on one of the babies that came yesterday. It was pinned to her blanket."

"It's a map. So what?"

"It's not just a map, Wren. Look at the arrows. It's a plan."

I stare until my vision blurs and the lines become a jumbled mess.

"That's our beach." Beck taps a section of the paper with a jagged nail.

"Is that . . . the Mainland?" I point to the map's only other landmass. It's not labeled.

"I don't know." Beck sighs. "Probably. Does it look two days away?"

I study the page for clues—anything that indicates that it's the Mainland. Anything to demarcate the Colony operating secretly within it. I'm distracted by the vastness of the ocean. Ninety percent of the map is blue.

Beck hastily folds the paper and claps it into my hand. "Right now, focus on defense."

I stagger back, my legs liquid. "Okay."

Beck shifts her supply bag to the other shoulder. "Come on." She nods downhill. "We gotta go. The Colony's waiting."

I push away from the rock and follow, pausing to take a quick look over my shoulder. A hawk flies over the Westside Forest. There's no sign of any others.

When we round the corner, I turn to Beck. "Should I be scared?"

"We should always be scared," she replies. "Scared and ready."

We join the others and assemble into a long line toward the beach. The necklace around my neck is heavy as lead.

CHAPTER 3

Section 2.4 - Head counts are mandatory and must be regularly executed to track and monitor activity on the Hill.

NOVA REMOVES HER shoes and hauls the first of four boats into the water, avoiding a floating gillnet. Ember gnaws on a piece of driftwood. The rest of us crowd along the golden arc of sand as if we're about to serenade the Departing Girls.

"A little help here?" Nova hollers, stumbling knee-deep through the water, the boat wedged on a sandbar only a few feet from shore. One by one, the Departing Girls wade into the water. I don't realize I'm hanging onto Sloan until she pulls her hand free of my grip. She's a Mother, and even though she's not mine, her pending departure unnerves me.

Beck trudges from boat to boat, checking the fuel gauges. *Is this how it was for her too? Did the former Head Girl leave her behind with a brand-new batch of babies and warnings of impending doom?* I swallow my fear, guiding it down my throat as if it's something tangible, a pit I'll never be able to digest. When I return my hand to my side, another picks it up—a tiny hand, half the size of my own. It belongs to Arrow. She's only three, technically still a Small, but she was assigned to the Collectors early because she was always getting into things and protesting naptime. Separated from the rest of the Smalls and her mother, I became her unofficial "Collector Mother."

I squeeze her hand, and she looks up at me, her face dirty and her belly protruding like a fat seabird's beneath her tulip-printed tank top. She smiles, her eyes dark and zealous. Someone has tied her hair into a little red knot on top of her head. It tugs at her eyes and stretches the Colony marking on the back of her neck.

"Are they going to turn into birds when they reach the Mainland?" she asks.

"No." I laugh. "At least, I don't think so."

She furls her brows in disappointment, takes back her hand, and crosses her arms high on her chest.

At the end of the beach, a pair of girlfriends say goodbye. They wipe away tears between mournful kisses and a hug that seems to stop time. Eventually, Beck whistles and one pulls away, the water lapping at the tattered hem of her dress. The other drops to her knees, lovesick, heartbroken. We all feel it. I glance at Quinn, who's fiddling with the tangled gillnet and pretending not to notice.

Minutes pass. Foragers check fish traps; a Small attempts a handstand and crumbles into a heap. I make a visor with my hand, shielding my eyes from the sun and noting that all four boats are programmed and loaded, their engines propelling them out to open water, spitting and sputtering in imperfect unison. A derelict oil rig looms in the distance, tilted and rusted orange, found property of the Colony. Only yesterday, black smoke billowed from its platform, announcing the arrival of four new babies. Quinn had rolled her eyes at the sight.

On the beach, we wave, some of us with both arms, desperate. We don't let up until we can't differentiate between the boats and the seagulls. Until the horizon has swallowed them. I pick up Arrow and set her on my hip. She plays with the Head Girl necklace dangling from my neck, touching each attachment. She also wears a necklace, a long chain that drapes below her rib cage with a pea-sized rock that emits an annoying shine. Her first find. Her small hands making work of the Hill's darkest corners.

Arrow wipes her nose on my new shirt and presses her chest into mine. The cadence of her heartbeat is quick, and mine speeds up in response. The sea is empty now. There is no sign of the girls who left, and I feel alone, surrounded by the twenty-nine who remain.

"Let's go," I finally yell, moving across the beach with Arrow still strapped to my front. I pass a Small with tiny braids, feet bare and brown as chestnuts, eating sand. "Where is her Mother?"

A young girl, fresh into the double digits, raises her hand and plods through the sand with two Smalls trailing behind her at a dismal pace. "Quinn, help this Mother out."

Quinn looks simultaneously incensed and repelled, hovering over the Small before setting down her spear and washing the girl's tongue with her shirt.

I step onto the dirt path that leads uphill, move Arrow to my other hip, and glance back at the line winding behind me. Quinn, still on the beach, files in at the rear, the offending Small patched into the line somewhere far away from her.

I consider Beck's instruction to assign more girls to nighttime defense and try to determine who and how many, but I can't even place who has what Assignment. I set Arrow down and make her walk. She fusses, takes a few clumsy steps, and reaches for me to pick her up again.

"No," I tell her. "You're a big girl. You need to walk."

She sticks out her bottom lip and slogs behind me. I massage my vacated shoulders. She weighs more than the microwave I pulled out of the Hill. I watch her bend to observe something in the grass and slip further behind, toward the back of the line.

At the Rock halfway up the hill, I pick up the Manual that Beck left behind from the Departure Ceremony and tuck it under my arm. Someone in line sings, drowning out the sounds of heavy breathing and scuffing feet.

We reach the outside of the Quarters, avoiding the piles of discarded shovels and pickaxes that line the shelter like unlit bonfires. Girls stop to drink water, waiting for the back half of the line to catch up. Mess is scattered everywhere from the Departure meal—unwashed plates and utensils, abandoned hunting gear, clothes, tears.

"Clean this up." I gesture, glancing at the sun's position. "We break out in fifteen."

I carry the Manual inside the Quarters through the elongated front room, which bends with the curve of the hill, toward the back of the structure. Letters and numbers line the wall where the Smalls sleep. A mirror, cracked and patched, is tucked into an alcove. The makeshift beds of the Departed Girls lie empty or have been dismantled. Ghost beds, ghost girls. I take a piece of foam from Nova's bed. It's only a few inches thick and the size of my torso, but it trumps my current set-up, which is a puke-stained comforter and a piece of plywood. I find a strand of her blonde hair entangled in the foam.

I dump the foam on the bed that I often share with Quinn and continue to a rear storage room. The ceiling is low; only Smalls can walk through without stooping. At the back of the room is an exit to the Westside Forest, an escape route. But it's blocked off. It has never been used. Beck's words replay in my head. *We should always be scared.* I touch the tunnel's makeshift wall and shrug. The only thing you ever need to escape is the midnight tears of new babies. It's amazing what you can use to plug your ears.

I set the Manual on top of a trunk and careen back through the minefield of beds to the outside, where evidence of breakfast has been virtually swallowed.

"Bravo," I announce, kicking a deer femur out of the way. "Back to work."

Girls obediently assemble into their assigned groups. The Collectors arm themselves with their tools, shovels slung over shoulders, cords wound and stakes bundled, and they head west downhill toward their current excavation site. The Mothers usher the Smalls into the Quarters for naptime. The Smalls rub their tired eyes and stumble in zigzags. One face-plants through the opening and screams at a mind-numbing pitch until her Mother sets her back on her feet and wipes the dust from her knees.

Quinn steps over a faceless stuffed bear wearing a tiny striped T-shirt. "You got that knife on you?"

I check my pocket. "Which one?"

"Ivory handle, blade about this long." She measures with her hands the width of a Small's head.

I nod toward the Quarters. "Under the bed."

"Thanks." She kicks the bear out of the way and disappears inside.

The remaining Hunters converge at the edge of the forest. Lennon coaches a younger girl on how to better handle her bow, pushing the girl's elbow up with a pair of fingers and repositioning her shoulders.

Quinn returns from the Quarters with the knife. "I'll give it back later," she says, shoving it in a sheath bulging with arrows. She pauses. "You okay?"

I nod, unconvinced.

"Chin up, then." She smiles. "You're the Head Girl now. Gotta look the part." She winks and charges off.

I don't want her to go. I wave, but her back is already to me.

I linger outside the Quarters, waiting for the Smalls to fall asleep so I can go back and get the Record. I need to move the profiles of the Departed Girls to the back of the binder and review the Assignments of those who remain. The Quarters goes quiet, only to explode seconds later with a full-body cry.

I wince, pick up the bear in the striped T-shirt, and take it inside. The Smalls are out of control, ransacking the place. One sits on my bed, picking apart the foam I salvaged from Nova. I snatch it away, and she kicks me in response. Another is sucking on the end of a wrench, causing a waterfall of rust-tainted drool to pour down her chin.

"Gross. Go lie down. Take this." I snatch the wrench and hand her the stuffed animal.

A Mother with a baby strapped to her back bends over a bed and combs the sparse bangs of another. Despite the chaos, the baby is almost asleep. As I back away, though, I step on someone's hand. There is silence, followed by a deafening scream.

I pick up the frantic baby and shove her face into the puffed letters of my shirt. "Sorry, sorry, sorry," I recite, examining her hand and brushing away the wavy lines of my bootprint. I kiss her knuckles. Her features are small—eyes sunken, hair thin. She's underweight. The screaming ensues, snot bubbling from her nose like water boiling. I turn to another Mother, a dark-skinned girl with perfectly symmetrical cornrows that gather in a tidy bundle at the nape of her neck. "Abena." I point to the screaming child hanging off my neck. "Who is her Mother?"

Abena gives me a weary glance as she hustles the Small who was eating the wrench onto a mattress. "Harlow," she says, sticking a wad of cloth under the girl's head as a pillow.

I look around the room for Harlow, the gaunt nine-year-old with the pinecone-colored hair and a gap between her front teeth wide enough to pass a shoe-lace through. She's nowhere. I carry the baby—who's now hyperventilating—outside and sit her on the grass. She topples over onto her side and puts her foot in her mouth. "Stay there."

I survey the Hill, but there's no sign of Harlow, only a few Suppliers cleaning ash from the firepit.

Abena appears at the entrance to the Quarters. "I'll take her now," she says, scooping up the sickly baby with the sallow skin and waif-like limbs. "Come on, Anouk. It's time to sleep." She disappears through the open-ing, cradling Anouk's head, the faint sound of humming trailing behind her like a musical shadow.

I cup my hands around my mouth and yell Harlow's name so loud I see stars. There's no one close enough to answer. I pace, inhaling and exhaling, trying to recall section 4.7 of the Manual, the part we always skim over, which details what to do when something "unexpected happens." Remain calm. Breathe. I lean against the Quarters, dizzy with adrenaline, waiting for the noise of the Smalls to dissipate.

When it does, I return like a Hunter, stealthy and silent. The babies are asleep, the Mothers lined up and seated against the wall like they've just run for their lives and collapsed. Abena doesn't blink. The other two pass a jar of water between them.

"So none of you know where Harlow is?"

One of the Mothers finishes the water and sets down the jar. "She was here this morning."

"What about the Departure Ceremony?"

"Yep," Abena says. "She sat in the back because Anouk was fussing."

"What about the beach? Anyone see her on the beach?"

The Mothers pause, squinting as though the answer lies in tiny print on the opposite wall.

"I think so?" Abena offers.

"Yeah," says another. "I watched her roll up her pants before going in the water."

"Did she come back out?"

"Of course she did. She waded in to launch one of the boats while I stayed with the Smalls."

I exhale, frustrated. "I'm going to the beach to look for her. In the meantime, Abena, as the new Lead Mother, take care of her Assignments. Or work it out between the three of you."

Abena twists her lips into a cynical knot. I can't blame her. The Mothers are outnumbered by the Smalls.

I back out of the Quarters, my mind racing like a girl trying to get to the front of the line but unable to locate where the line is. Maybe Harlow left. Maybe she pushed the boat out and climbed aboard. Never. Ridiculous. Beck would have thrown her back to shore. She'd be sentenced to the shed for thirty days; it would be my responsibility to enforce it, to take away her belongings, and use the switch. I shudder. "Harlow," I holler, passing the remnants of last month's excavation site, bare and staked, the way it will look for months until the grass returns, masking the scent of decay and concealing the earth beneath it like a shroud.

Why didn't I do a head count? It's the first thing I should've done before we dispersed for work. A few hours on the job and I've already screwed up. I yank the flower from my hair and toss it on the path. As I get closer to the beach, the air smells like it's been filtered through a whale carcass. Gag.

I skid down the remainder of the trail, landing on my knees in the sand. The beach is empty, but there's an opening in the rock cliff where the fishing gear is stored. I check for Harlow inside. Piles of nets and tangled fishing line litter the floor. A few spears are stacked in the corner beside a single corroded flipper, too large to fit anyone. Someone painted a fish on the wall.

I step back onto the beach and trip on a buoy. "Harlow!"

Only my echo answers, frightened, almost unrecognizable. I cup water in my hands and rub it through my hair to cool off and stagger back uphill to look for Quinn. I find her en route to the Quarters with blood on her cheek.

"Hey."

"You're panting," she observes.

I take a deep breath. "A Mother is missing."

"Which one?"

"Harlow."

"The skinny kid with the messed-up teeth. She got holes in her ears?"

"Yeah, her."

"Where is she?"

"If I knew, then she wouldn't be missing, would she?"

Quinn looks around the Hill as if Harlow may be somewhere obvious and out in the open. "Did you check the beach?"

"Yes, I checked the beach. Why do you think I'm panting?"

A Supplier with a shaved head shuffles by with a pot, water sloshing out the sides.

"You check the well?"

"Mothers don't get water."

"Maybe the babies were thirsty. I could hear them from the forest."

I sigh.

Quinn whittles her spear into the ground. "What did the other Mothers say?"

"Nothing. They saw her help push one of the boats out to sea."

Quinn shrugs. "Betcha she's just hiding from the babies. Probably needed a break. I would if I was a Mother. New babies are the worst, and the Smalls are crazy. Am I bleeding?" She thrusts her cheek forward.

"Yes." I flash back to the mayhem of naptime.

Quinn pats her cheek with the inside of her wrist. "Do a head count, Wren. She'll come back."

It's the last thing I want to do, seeing as I just sent everyone away. I don't even know which direction the Foragers went. "Might as well go get your girls."

Quinn responds with a tweak of her eyebrows and heads back toward the Westside Forest while I go to the Rock. Ember bounds beside me encouragingly and then runs off. The adrenaline coursing through my legs makes my steps long and sloppy. I scramble to the top of the boulder, skinning my knees on the way up, and then whistle three times, holding each blow until my diaphragm hurts and my head trembles like a twanged bow.

Girls emerge from all directions. The Mothers seethe and stumble, loaded with drowsy Smalls. The Collectors exchange confused glances and cling to their shovels. One of them holds a find under her arm—some kind of pipe. The Foragers can't help but pick things along the way.

"What's with the head count?" one of them asks.

"Quiet," Quinn yips.

"You be quiet," she throws back. "We just got to the work site. Why didn't we do this earlier?"

I put my hand in the air. "Head count."

There's a moment of silence. Anarchy is expunged through dramatic sighs and is replaced with cooperation, everyone shuffling into a line that's akin to a rainbow. A Supplier with a curvy mid-section and pink cheeks shouts, "One." The numbers follow in line. Arrow stands at the end, swinging a sawed-off rake around recklessly. The girl before her repeats her number and snatches away the tool.

"Twenty-eight," Arrow growls.

I say, "twenty-nine," but it comes out like a question. I should be thirty. "Do it again."

The curvy girl starts over and bumps her hip into number two. I follow along in my head. Seven, nineteen, twenty-three. I don't say my number, which is still twenty-nine. "One more time."

A Hunter says, "We know how to count." A pair of dead squirrels drapes from ties around her neck.

"Shush," I spit.

"One," says the curvy girl.

"Twenty-eight," finishes Arrow.

Quinn steps out of line and tears over to the Rock. "Wren, it's not going to change. It's twenty-nine."

"Who's missing?" someone asks.

Abena replies, "Harlow."

A Supplier fidgets, unable to keep still, swinging her leg back and forth. "Where is she?"

Harlow is missing. Less than half a day in charge, and I've already screwed up.

CHAPTER 4

Section 2.2 – Outside of the Hill's boundary, girls cannot survive.

I GAPE AT the girls with their dirty faces and gnarly hair. "As you were. Except for the Hunters. You stay."

"As you were?" Abena gestures to the bleary-eyed children at her feet. "Right." She trudges toward the Quarters, herding the Smalls. Anouk shrieks like her feet are scream-activated. Quinn plugs her ears. In the distance, Ember paces the edge of the forest, bounding and barking intermittently.

I surf down the side of the rock and nearly plow Quinn over.

"Now what are you going to do?" she asks, sharpening her knife on a river stone, the blade screeching.

I try to portray an impression of Head Girl calm, chin up like Quinn suggested, shoulders poised. I don't want her to sense my fear, though I wear it like a badge. Hunters love fear. It makes them feel bigger than they are. The minute I appear weak, Quinn will start a revolution. She wouldn't be able to stop herself.

"For starters, get someone to take your place."

She studies me for a minute, fixes her dark eyes on my single unblinking one. Two on one. She seems both impressed and irritated by my tone, which is stern and necessary. All business. We have an audience. She plays along.

"Pick Blue," I whisper, referring to the blonde nicknamed after a previous stint with hypothermia.

Quinn nods. "Blue," she hollers over her shoulder. "You're in charge. Go to the cliff and gather some rocks. Big ones." She gestures, as though her hands are wrapped around an invisible head. Her fingernails are black. She faces me again. Together, we watch Blue lead the Hunters toward the cliff. "Maybe she did go to the Mainland."

"You know if she tried to board one of those boats, Beck would have thrown her off."

Quinn shrugs. "What if it was by accident?"

"How do you accidentally get on a boat without anyone noticing?"

"She was small. Maybe she fell in when she was pushing, wriggled her way under someone's pack."

"She hated the water," I argue. "She barely passed her swim module."

Quinn considers this, wipes sweat from her upper lip, and turns to view the blackened Eastside Forest. "Well, she's got to be here somewhere. No one just leaves."

"Tora."

Quinn rolls her eyes. "That was nearly fifteen years ago. She doesn't count. Did you check Harlow's bed? Is her stuff still here?"

"No," I reply, already walking in the direction of the Quarters.

"No, you didn't check, or no, her stuff's not there?"

"No," I snap, "as in I haven't even had the chance to look."

Quinn grabs my wrist, rough but affectionate. "Calm down, Wren. Didn't she miss a head count once before? Like a month ago?"

"She was late once, but she blamed it on one of the Smalls."

"Bloody Smalls. Can't stand them."

"Quinn."

"Sorry, they won't stop crying. That Anouk never shuts up."

"It's not her fault. I don't think she's well." We walk in silence, our feet scuffing up the worn path, and I think of the sightings Beck warned of. Could Harlow have been . . . abducted? No. It's a possibility I don't want to consider—I *can't* consider. "Ever see anything weird when you're out hunting?"

Ember trots over, her head high, mug damp. I pet her side.

"Depends on what kind of weird we're talking. I saw a two-headed snake once."

"Anything else?"

"You're a Collector—sorry, *were* a Collector. You're the ones who find all the weird stuff." She kicks a rock up the path. "Remember that time you found the bald plastic person with the red cheeks and fancy lashes?"

"It was missing an arm."

"Or the shoe with the spiky heel?"

"I'm not even convinced that was a shoe."

Quinn shrugs. "Better than the shoe with the blade."

"You mean the 'hockey skate.'"

"The skate, yeah. Actually, it wasn't that bad once we figured out how to remove the blade."

"Can you go check the Quarters to see if Harlow's stuff is there?"

Quinn nods and runs ahead, slowing as the Hill steepens. My mind races behind her. The knot atop my head unravels. Where is Harlow? I think of all the places where she could have gotten caught up, stuck, swept away. Culled by a root. Pinned by a rock. Swallowed by an undertow.

I veer off course to check the Shed—a small enclosure, with a rickety door and a wooden latch. The hinges creak as I fling it open. There's nothing inside except mushrooms blooming through the floorboards, and perhaps Quinn's guilt. She was the last one to be sentenced to it after falling asleep on watch—twice in one night.

I push the door closed and maneuver the latch into the locked position, the frame warped and split. When I reach the entrance to the Quarters, I bump into Quinn coming out. "Her stuff is still there. One measuring tape, a ceramic brooch, and a heap of raggedy clothes."

I turn away from her and exhale into the first discernable breeze of the day. I don't tell her about the sightings—the *others*. Nor do I tell her about my gut feeling, which is dark and ominous. "I should check the Record. Gimme my knife."

Quinn pulls it from her pants pocket, and I jam the blade under the clasp of the trunk where the Record is stored. The clasp pops open. Quinn throws back the top, and I pull out the book. Beck has already moved the Departed Girls to the back, leaving my profile at the front. I flip the pages rapidly, not wanting Quinn to see anything private written about me by a previous Head Girl.

She exhales a weighted sigh. "As if you have anything to hide."

I continue flipping until I reach Harlow's record. *Arrival #211. Fair hair, medium skin. Holes in earlobes. Petite.* The entry continues in a different color. *Assignment: Mother. Quiet but attentive. Physically not very strong. Good with the Smalls.*

"Well, that was helpful." Quinn picks her teeth with a broken shell from her pocket. "And what's with the holes in her ears?"

"I don't know. That's all it says."

"Reminds me of Priya. Remember how she was missing the tip of her pinkie?"

I drop the Record back into the trunk and close the lid. "Barely. She departed right after I arrived."

Quinn flicks the shell onto the floor. "You suppose Harlow just got lost?"

"How could she get lost? She's nine. It's not like she doesn't know her way around. There are only so many places to go."

"No kidding. It's like living in a fishbowl."

"I don't know what that is."

"Something my Mother told me. People used to keep fish in little glass bowls, so the fish just swam in circles." She twirls her finger.

"What's that have to do with Harlow?"

Quinn puts her hands up defensively, and I realize I was yelling. I take a step toward her like it might turn down my volume.

"Maybe she went looking for a new water source." Quinn crosses her arms. "You see how backed up the laundry is?"

I shake my head. "The well's fine and the Westside stream still has a decent flow."

"Well, it's not like there are a whole lot of possibilities here."

"What if she was taken?"

She places her hand over my mouth. I push it away, but she grabs my wrist.

"What?" I shake myself free, her handprint still visible on my forearm.

"Don't even suggest that."

"But what if it's true? What if someone knows we're here? Isn't it possible?"

"No one knows we're here. But if you say stuff like that, people will panic."

"You think there's a chance, don't you?"

She stares back at me, fear in her eyes.

"Quinn, there's stuff you don't know." My voice wavers.

"Like what?'

"Just . . . Beck said there was disorder on the Mainland."

"The Manual says the same thing. We know this already, Wren. It's a bloody mess out there, but girls have been on this Hill for sixty-six years."

"Sixty-seven."

"Fine, sixty-seven, and no one's ever just popped by to say hello or ask if they could borrow a shovel or offer us a ride on a luxury raft."

"Are you sure about that?"

Quinn's eyes shift.

"Quinn?"

She yanks me violently by the arm until we're inches apart. "I saw something once," she whispers, but it sounds more like a growl. Her dark lashes are askew, and she doesn't blink.

"What? What did you see?"

"I saw someone, but it wasn't one of us. In fact, they looked nothing like us."

"What do you mean?" I clear my throat and lie. "No one's ever reported seeing anyone out there." I gesture toward the Eastside Forest.

"Because I didn't report it."

"What do you mean, you didn't report it? Why?"

Quinn looks behind her. "Because I was told not to."

"By who?"

"Odessa."

"Odessa? Why would she say that?" I lower my voice

when one of the Smalls stirs on the floor. "Did she not believe you?"

"Because she saw it too."

A Collector girl with a split lip appears at the entry-way of the Quarters. "Excuse me," she says, not waiting to be invited in. "My Mother sent me to tell you that Arrow keeps repeating Harlow's name and pointing to the forest."

"The forest?" I ask, alarmed. "Which one—the West-side or Eastside?"

"Eastside."

"Thanks." I swallow the lump in my throat. "I'll talk to Arrow in a minute." I watch the girl turn and bolt down the hill from where she came.

"That makes no sense." I look at Quinn. "Why would Harlow go into the Eastside Forest? It's pitch-black— you can't even walk through it."

Quinn rolls her eyes. "You're believing an eyewitness account from Arrow? She's three years old. Yesterday, I caught her talking to her foot."

"She's imaginative, yes, but she's also smart. And she's a Collector. She would've at least had the opportunity to see something."

"But the Collectors were working in the Westside Forest today. How could she have seen anything in the Eastside?"

I pause. "I don't know, but right now we've got nothing else to go on. We know Harlow was at the Departure Ceremony and we know she helped push one of the boats into the water." I tug at my ponytail. "You were at the end of the line when we left the beach—do you remember seeing her somewhere in front of you?"

"I think so." Quinn's expression changes from certainty to doubt. "I remember her carrying one of the Smalls, but there was one point when I had to leave the line to go back and get my spear."

"You forgot your spear?"

She hugs it to her chest. "You made me help out that Small who was eating sand. I had to put it down."

"So there's a possibility that Harlow went missing at some point *after* we left the beach but *before* we returned to our Assignments."

"Yes," she concludes reluctantly. "There's a possibility."

"We have to talk to Arrow." I start downhill.

"Wren," Quinn says from behind me. "That time with Odessa? What we saw wasn't a girl."

I stop mid-stride and spin to face her. "What do you mean? Was it some kind of animal?"

"Odessa said it was a boy."

"On the Hill?"

"That's what she said."

"Where?"

"Way back in the Westside Forest. He was following a game trail."

I continue down, my speed increasing with each elongated step. "How could you have never told me this before?"

"Why didn't you show me the map Beck gave you at the Departure Ceremony?"

I stop. "How do you know about that?"

Quinn turns away.

"You were spying, weren't you? Whore."

"Whore? Huh?"

"I don't know. My Mother said it once when she was really mad."

"Is that in the Manual?"

"Never mind the Manual. What did he look like?"

"He looked like the pictures in the appendix, but he was built like a tree. Wide shoulders. Tall. Long hair."

"Did he have a weapon?"

"A bow."

"Did he try to rape you?"

"No! Wren, come on." Her cheeks flourish red.

"What? You know what the Manual says."

"We were in a hunting blind."

Arrow comes into view, thumb in her mouth, just south of the Rock.

"I still don't understand why you didn't report it."

Quinn bites her lip. "Okay, we weren't in a hunting blind. We followed a game trail past the boundary. Odessa had seen a deer; we were starving. It was winter. You know what would have happened if Beck had found out."

"The Shed."

"For me, maybe. I was only ten. Odessa would have been banished."

"You should have killed him."

CHAPTER 5

Section 2.8 — Do not go into the Eastside Forest.

ARROW DRINKS SOUP from a bowl, flanked by Collectors double her size. When she's lapped up all the broth, she uses her hands to scoop out the curled greens and chunks of whitefish. A Forager tosses me a blackberry.

"Use your spoon, Arrow."

"Done." She wipes her chin with her bare arm, sits proudly back on her heels and gnaws on a piece of rye bread. Ember tries to lick her face, and she bats her away.

"Come here, girl." I eat the berry and sit on the ground, where Arrow crawls over and rests her head against my chest. She plays with the tiny rock hanging from the chain around her neck, rolls it between her thumb and pointer finger. Her eyes are heavy.

"Since when are you into naptime?" I rouse her from her reclined position, bounce her on my knee. Her head falls forward. I brush away the damp strings of hair that have fallen out of her knot and stick to her sweaty forehead. "Where's Harlow?" I whisper, trying not to arouse the interest of the others.

"Forest."

"Did you see her go into the forest?"

She nods and pulls from a satchel tied around her waist a rock similar to the one dangling from her neck, except this one is blue and much bigger. About the size of my thumbnail.

"Where did you find this?" I take it in the palm of my hand. The edges are scuffed, and there's a hole whittled through the middle. A bead. "That all you find today? No old quilts or rubber tires or glasses?"

She shrugs and closes her eyes.

"Not yet," I say again, noting that the toenail she lost on a previous dig is finally growing back in. "Which forest did Harlow go into? The one by the hunting grounds, or the beach one?"

"Beach." She yawns, exposing a mishmash of crooked teeth.

"Did she walk in? Was she alone?"

Arrow yawns again and shakes her head no.

"No, she wasn't alone, or no, she didn't walk?" I sit up straighter now, every muscle in my body constricted, my mouth dry.

"No," she repeats.

I separate the questions, reminding myself she's only three. "Was she alone?"

"Yes," Arrow answers.

"Did she walk into the forest?"

"No." She shakes her head and begins to fuss.

I rub Arrow's back. Why would Harlow crawl into the woods? Unless she was sick and had to vomit, brought to her knees by fever or flu or spoiled food. I think of last night's crickets, nutty and charred, and I pick at a seed wedged between my teeth and shiver. She would not just run away, slipping out of line, crawling to escape detection. Even a mention of the Eastside Forest made her cry. The Manual terrified her. And if she *had* just upped and walked away like Tora, someone would have seen her. Someone would have stopped her, hauled her back by her hair. I begin to think Quinn is right and wonder why I believe a three-year-old.

A bird the size of my fist pecks at the ground and retreats. Maybe Harlow took Quinn's spear knowing Quinn would have to go back for it, and when she did, she crawled away undetected. No one was watching the back of the line. There was opportunity. But why? Unless she wanted to die. Occasionally, some girls wanted to.

I shift my position and look at Arrow. "So, Harlow crawled in?"

Arrow shakes her head. "On her back."

"Wait a minute." I prop her on my lap, so she's directly in front of me and blow in her face. She winces. "Look at me. What do you mean, *on her back*?"

She taps her shoulder blade. I'm confused.

"Like this." Arrow climbs off my lap and lies next to me on the grass. Her legs stretch out so that her knees fall to the side and she extends her arms over her head.

"That's impossible," I say. "You can't move like that."

Arrow sighs in frustration and closes her eyes.

Quinn nudges me from behind with her knee, and I jump. "Quinn, don't do that. You scared me."

She rests her chin on my shoulder and whispers in my ear, "You can move like that if you're being dragged."

CHAPTER 6

Section 8.3 — If you encounter a boy, take swift and violent action to eliminate him.

I SCRAMBLE TO my feet. "I need everyone here."

"Now?"

"Yes, now." I whistle three times, shrill and sloppy. I can barely breathe.

The girls stop eating. "What's going on?"

"Harlow."

A Forager arriving from uphill jams a handful of roots into her sack. "You check the Shed? She's probably inside hiding from the babies. The one with the little spike of hair never shuts up."

"She's not in the Shed," I say. "She's not in the Quarters, or on the beach, or in the Westside Forest. She's nowhere."

A Collector says, "Maybe she just went—"

"She's not here!" I yell. "What don't you understand?"

The Collector attempts to speak, but Quinn raises a hand.

"I have to find her." My voice cracks.

"Where exactly do you plan on looking?" A Hunter examines the tip of her spear, her hair loose around her face. More girls arrive.

I stare at the Eastside Forest.

"You've got to be joking," a Mother says. "You can't."

A Forager smashes a walnut, causing the shell to shatter. "No way Harlow would've gone in there."

My nose tingles, signaling the rise of tears. I fight it. "I don't think it was by choice."

The Hill goes quiet. Even the Smalls sense there's something wrong.

Someone in the crowd says, "You can't just *leave*."

"She's only nine."

I face the black wall of the Eastside Forest again. There's no reasonable point of entry. No obvious place to search. I imagine it will be like walking into another dimension, a nightmare, the Mainland.

A Mother stands up. "*Leaving the boundary places the Hill and Colony at risk of discovery and harm.*' Section 5.3."

Balancing on a stump, Lennon recites: "*Girls over the age of ten caught attempting to leave the Hill will be stripped of their identity, banished from the Colony, and sent to the Mainland.*' Section 5.4."

"*Outside of the Hill's boundary, girls cannot survive.*' Section 2.2," Abena adds.

Girls cannot survive. "Section 6.0," I retort. "*To maintain order, the Head Girl must be obeyed at all times during her tenure. Those found to question her authority'* . . . need I go on?"

A girl with dark skin and curls like frayed rope hands off her empty plate and crosses her legs. "Does that mean Quinn is in charge while you're gone?"

Across from me, Quinn tosses bits of dried fruit into the air, catching them on her tongue. We all watch. Knowing she has an audience, she pierces a fig on the end of a knife and eats it off the tip. The sight of the sharp metal against her bottom lip makes me shiver—her intent, no doubt. She stands with one foot planted on a rock, already planning her first command.

"No." I clutch the knife in my pocket. "Quinn won't be in charge."

Quinn clenches her teeth, the vein on her forehead pulsing in protest. She's the second oldest. It's her who should be left in charge. We all know the rules.

"She won't be left in charge, because she's coming with me."

The expression on Quinn's red-hot face changes from anger to suspicion to curiosity to satisfaction, all within five seconds, all of it communicated by her shifting eyes.

"I need a skilled Hunter."

Girls shrug, accepting my explanation, even if it's only a half-truth. I need an experienced Hunter, but I also just need her. I need her to tell me we'll be okay, even if it's a lie. Especially if it's a lie.

Blue, who's arrived unnoticed with an armload of

rocks, looks from girl to girl, trying to make sense of the situation.

"Blue, you'll take Quinn's place as Lead Hunter, and Clover, you'll take mine."

Clover freezes, her spoon midway to her mouth. "Me?"

"Yes, you. You're exempt from your collecting duties until I return. Blue will help out during free time."

Blue glances at Clover, who returns her spoon, along with the uneaten soup, back to the bowl.

"Does everyone understand?"

A scattered *yes* comes from the crowd. Dishes and utensils are collected. Woven mats are hand-brushed clean. Quinn polishes her spear.

"One more thing," I say. "Don't go near the Eastside Forest."

"Are we in danger?" This question comes from a six-year-old. Her legs jut out from beneath her in opposite directions. She has striped socks that end just above her knees. Her face is soft, as though she was painted into existence.

"We're always in danger. You know that. Section 3.3—'*uprisings on the Mainland are common, unpredictable, and violent.*'"

I dismiss everyone except for Blue and Clover. We join Quinn by an old firepit while the girls disperse. Clover rocks back and forth, head down and fingers interlocked.

"What?"

"I don't know how to be the Leader," she blurts.

"You'll be fine. Just do what I did. "

"Except don't lose anyone," Quinn adds.

I glare at her. "You want to stay here?"

Clover fidgets. I lift her chin with my finger, forcing her to look me in the eye. "Stick to the routine. I chose you because I know you can do that."

She nods, but her head barely moves against the resistance of my finger. Truth is, I picked her because she's obedient and will follow the rules. Paranoid. I'll have a job when I return to the Hill, which is something I'm not sure of if I leave Quinn behind. The Manual describes a previously attempted coup. A girl like Quinn—loud and intimidating and charismatic in a bad way—tried to take over, staged a revolution in the middle of the night, and locked the Head Girl in the Shed.

Quinn is the kind of girl you need to keep close. The kind you take with you when you leave.

"I don't know how long we'll be gone. We're taking supplies for three days—four if we ration conservatively."

Clover shifts her weight from one foot to the other. "Four days? Are you mad? You'll never survive out there."

"Well, we're going to try. And you'll survive here."

She takes a deep breath and exhales. Blue stands beside her, working a burr out of her hair. "Good luck," Clover mutters.

"We're leaving shortly. No big goodbyes, no tears, no ceremonies. We're just going to slip away like we're going for water."

"No way you're slipping through *those* trees," Blue snorts, a smug look on her narrow face. I ignore her.

"Is Harlow going to be in trouble? When you find her?" Clover asks.

"Yeah, she'll be in trouble," Quinn says.

My cheeks flush. It's my decision whether Harlow gets punished, not Quinn's. I can hardly give Harlow the switch or toss her in the Shed if she was dragged away against her will. "That depends."

Quinn scoffs.

"Because you might not find her?" Clover asks.

"No. Because we—*I*—don't know the circumstances of her disappearance."

Quinn drags Blue by the arm. "I'll meet you at the Quarters."

I nod, and she carries on up the Hill.

The baby hair around Clover's forehead stands at attention with worry. She has a handful of freckles that form an elongated version of the Big Dipper across the bridge of her nose. "Did someone take her? Was it a boy? Do they know we're here?"

I lift my patch and move closer. The sight of my exposed right eye makes her breath gallop, and she covers her mouth as though that might be able to silence it. Then she drops her hand and recovers her breath. My eye looks normal. I've seen my reflection in the water and in the shards of mirror we dig up from the Hill. She's the first and only one to see my unpatched eye, a gesture of trust. Not even Quinn's seen it.

"I don't know." I return the patch to its place. "I'm still

hoping there's a reasonable explanation for why she's gone." I lean in even closer, so our lips are nearly touching. "But yes. There's a very real possibility she was abducted." My voice is so quiet I'm unsure if I've even said the words out loud. Confusion registers across Clover's brow.

"By a boy?"

"I'm not sure, Clover. For all I know, the Colony took her. Maybe this is all a test." A test I'm failing miserably.

She nods pensively.

"Just be careful. Avoid the Eastside Forest. Do head counts." I reach into my bag. "And take one of these." I hand her one of the Hill's two-way radios, keeping the other for myself. "The battery is low in both, and I'm not sure what the range will be out there." I nod toward the Eastside Forest. "Only use it in case of emergency."

Clover rolls the switch forward until the radio crackles to life. She fiddles with the volume and then turns it off.

"I can't leave Harlow out there alone. I don't want another Tora. Not when I'm in charge."

"But what if we see the Arrival Signal?"

"Highly unlikely." I sigh, wondering if I made the wrong choice in picking her to replace me. I can't decide if her questions are a good thing—a sign of scrupulousness and preparedness—or weakness and incompetence. "We just got babies the other day," I remind her. "It'll be a while before we start seeing Arrival Signals. Nine months, a year." I pause to check myself, to make sure what I'm saying is correct. But I'm right. I can't remember a time when Smalls arrived within a few months of each other, let alone days.

"Anouk came within a week of an arrival."

"Fine," I relent. "In the rare event you see an Arrival Signal, go to the beach and receive them, but I highly doubt there will be any Smalls arriving in the next three days." I wave three fingers in her face and notice dried blood on my knuckle. "Three days," I repeat. "Only three."

"Or four."

"At most."

"Fine," Clover says, throwing her hands up with reluctance. "Be safe." She tucks the radio into the waistband of her pants and wraps her calloused hands around mine, closing her eyes tight, as though she's trying to expel a bad memory. I watch and wait until she lets go of my hands and blinks. "I asked the forest to protect you," she explains. "And Quinn."

I kiss her cheek, right on the handle of the Big Dipper. "Thank you."

I don't think much of what she's said, but as I look at the forest sloping east from the Hill, the endless mass of blackened trees stretching for miles like unearthly hands, her prayer exacts a tinge of comfort. I head toward the Quarters; Clover, the firepit. What's left of her pink shirt flaps in the wind.

"Clover," I say, heart rate elevated. "Stop!"

She turns.

"Can you ask the forest to protect Harlow too?"

She bows in acknowledgment, and I run.

CHAPTER 7

Section 7.7 – ... slut, and bitch. Additional banned words are listed in Appendix C: PATRIARCHAL LANGUAGE.

I REACH THE Quarters out of breath. I grab my pack from beside my bed, my hands trembling as I re-tie my frayed laces. Quinn pushes a hammock out of the way and emerges from under it. It swings back and thumps her on the hip. She gives it a dirty look and then tightens the straps of her pack, which is already full and slung across her shoulders.

"The Suppliers have our food ready," she says.

"Go ahead. I'll be there in a minute."

She's changed into boots that lace up to her knees. They are too big. Foolish. We knock shoulders as she passes through the exit.

"Watch where you're going."

She sticks out her tongue. When she's out of view, I prop open the trunk with a knife. I take out a compass, which lies facedown in the corner of the trunk. The GPS watch is broken, no one able to fix it, the Colony unable to replace it. Why wouldn't they have sent new parts? An amendment to the Manual on how to fix it? They should have sent supplies with the babies: batteries, flint, some new books. I polish the compass with my shirt until I can make out the poles and stick it in my pocket.

I debate whether to bring the Record, since it's my responsibility to manage. I pick it up and flip through the yellowed pages, the writing faded and barely legible, especially the pages at the back. Hundreds of them. All girls who have gone. Then I close it and weigh it in my hand. It will only take up room in my pack, but before I can lower it safely back into the trunk, it topples. The metal-clawed rings keeping the papers together pop open like a jaw, causing the pages to fan out across the bottom of the trunk.

"Shit," I whine and do my best to push the papers into a stack. I don't have time to feed the drilled pages back into the metal rings, so I snap it shut and jam the papers in loose. As I set it back into the trunk, though, I notice pages I've missed.

They're smaller than the others and contain drawings. I flip through the first few. There's a moose, a few different species of birds, sketches of trees from the hunting grounds . . . and the last one is a boy, faceless, hulking. Different from the detailed sketch in the Manual. Different also from the boy Quinn described, but a boy nonetheless. Is it a portrait? A Mainland boy? A . . . Hill . . . boy?

My hand trembles.

"Are you coming?" Quinn shouts from behind me, Ember panting beside her.

I jump, fold the sketch in half, and stuff it into my pocket with the compass. I slip the remaining drawings into the Record.

"Got a compass." I clear my throat and tip the top of the trunk until gravity pulls it down with a resounding thud. "Let's go." I blow past Quinn, summoning Ember to my side. "Come here. Who's a good girl?"

Quinn trails and then rushes to catch up, so we're stride for stride.

"I know I said we wouldn't make a big deal about leaving, but I want to say goodbye to Arrow." I don't admit why. I don't tell Quinn I'm unsure we'll make it back.

"She's asleep."

I shut down with disappointment until we reach the edge of the Eastside Forest, half way down the hill. I blast two short whistles, a message to the girls that we're on our way. There's no response, not even a wind to bend the grass and make it swish. I step into the woods, chest tight, throat constricted like I've swallowed the night. Ember barks.

"Wait," Quinn shouts, both feet still planted firmly on the adjacent path. I step back, irritated that I'll have to re-take that first step, which was equal parts courageous and terrifying.

She links her pinkie with mine and slowly draws our joined hands upwards. Neither of us says anything, but the gesture conveys solidarity. Eventually, we let go, and after deep breaths like we're about to jump into icy water, we step into the Eastside Forest, weapons drawn.

THE UNDERBRUSH IS thick, forcing us to take exaggerated steps, lifting our knees to our hips. Only fifty paces in, we're already exhausted. And loud. Quinn scolds me for stepping on a branch, only to crack one seconds later. Hunting will prove useless. Any animal in a three-mile radius will have already fled. We'll be eating nothing but plants, like Lennon.

I steady myself with a branch as Ember forges ahead. There's nothing to suggest that Harlow—or anything, for that matter—passed through here. No obvious pathways, no markings, nothing other than trees with sharp needles and cones the size of kneecaps. We tear bits of yellow cloth from an old shirt excavated from the Hill and tie them to low-lying branches.

"What does the compass say?" Quinn pauses to drink from one of the water containers.

"You can't tell which direction we're traveling in?" I pull the compass out of my pocket, careful not to drop the sketch I took from the Record.

"I'm disoriented."

"We're still moving east."

It seems obvious; we've been walking on a complete slant, the hill sloping up from our left sides and down from beneath our bent right ankles. She hands me the water, and I take huge gulps. Wiping a drip from my chin, Quinn stares at me.

"What?"

"We don't have a plan," she says, whirling around, arms flailing.

"The plan is to find Harlow."

"Look around," she says. "We're surrounded by all these ridiculous plants or vines or whatever they are." She bats away a flying insect.

"Quinn, it's been less than an hour. You've stalked a mouse for longer than this."

"What, are we going to keep walking aimlessly until we find a clue?"

"Maybe," I say. "A clue. Or a feeling."

"A *feeling*? Remind me what section of the Manual I can find that filed under."

"Stop being such a—"

"Such a what, Wren?"

"A bitch," I blurt.

"Nice. If the Colony could only hear you now. The Head Girl using a forbidden word."

"I'm sorry. I'm just . . . I'm feeling overwhelmed. And you're not exactly being cooperative."

"Well, I *feel* like this is a waste of time. Look around you. We shouldn't be here. This was a bad decision. Let me know when you're ready to head back." She slaps at her neck and keeps moving.

I grab her arm and forget about being quiet, suddenly incensed. "How could you say this is a waste of time? I'm responsible for Harlow, and like it or not, as second-in-command, so are you."

"I didn't make her disappear."

"But you admitted that you left the back of the line when we were returning from the beach."

Her eyes narrow and shift, the way they always do when she feels under fire.

"We're going to keep searching for clues until nightfall and then we'll set up camp. We'll figure tomorrow out later."

I take another sip of water and wait for her reaction, but she's distracted, scanning the canopy of trees overhead. Like a Hunter.

"What?"

She puts her finger to her lips. I stand frozen and listen, trying to tap into my sense of sound, which is normally good. At the same time that Quinn whips her head around, I think I hear something. A faint rustling, like a branch that's been disturbed.

Seconds later, I hear it again, but I can't place it—can't even tell if it's coming from up above or at ground-level. Ember's ears perk with alarm. Quinn looks at me, wide-eyed, a leaf sticking out of her unruly black hair. "Did you hear that?"

I pick up her fear. It smells like the blood on my knuckle that I notice every time my arm swings forward.

"I didn't hear anything," I deny. If I admit it, she'll convince me she's right. That we shouldn't be here. That we should go back.

"You didn't hear that?" She squats down and waves her hand through the leaves and brush. "Like that."

"Nope. Didn't hear anything."

Ember lets out a succession of barks that end in a wolf-like howl.

"Shut up," Quinn scolds, straightening. "Why on earth would you bring her?"

"I couldn't have just left her behind. We're practically attached."

"You've only had her a few weeks."

"Sometimes that's all it takes."

A light wind moves through the treetops. A bird I can't identify flies from one branch to another. The sun blinds me, but I see a flicker of red wings. Then I hear the sound again—crumpling paper.

"There it is again." Quinn drives her spear into the ground.

"It's probably just a squirrel. Look at this place. It's gotta be teeming with them." As if on cue, a squirrel, black and fat, runs straight up the neighboring tree and disappears in a mass of branches. "See?"

She pulls the spear free, and we continue trekking through the brush, tagging trees as we pass, surveying the landscape for evidence. I'm not convinced what we heard was a squirrel, but I don't share this with Quinn. She's no good to me scared. It's enough to deal with my own fear, my own senses, my own doubt. Is she right? Is this a mistake? I turn and look behind me. There's no sign of the Hill. It's as if we've been swallowed into another world and the jaw has been wired shut.

After hours of hiking on a slant, we stop for a break. A downed tree provides the perfect place to sit and remove layers. My lower back throbs from walking at such an odd angle. I check the sky between the trees. "We've only got about an hour until dusk."

"I'm starving," Quinn replies, her cheeks gut-pink.

"Me too," I admit, aware of the emptiness in my stomach. "But we should wait until we set up camp."

Quinn looks up at the sky and nods, taking off her long-sleeved shirt and tying it around her waist. She opens the water, and we both take a few sips. I have to will myself to stand up again, kneading my lower back with my hands.

"I need another minute." I want to rest my head on her lap, but I don't. Quinn seems in no rush. She digs dirt out from the treads of her boots with a stick and airs out her armpits.

"We could have a few berries."

She points to a squat bush across from us. I can't remember what kind they are, but I recognize their peculiar purple color.

"We eat 'em all the time hunting." She plucks off a handful and holds them up in front of me. "Try one."

I take one and roll it between my thumb and forefinger. It's harder than I expected. Quinn places the rest in her mouth and closes her eyes. "They're a little tart," she musters between pursed lips. "Suppliers normally cook them."

I take a bite and shiver. It's sourer than I expected, and I shake my head in an attempt to make the taste disappear. "Way better cooked." I pour water into a tin cup and set it down for Ember. Quinn plucks off a few more berries.

"Catch." She tosses one in my direction. I open my mouth, but it bounces off my lip. "Try again," she laughs, holding the berry up to her eye and throwing it toward me. This one ricochets off my nose.

"Hey! That was a terrible shot."

A leggy spider sways in a web. I can tell by the markings that it's inedible.

"You moved." She takes another berry from her hand.

I sit with my mouth wide open and catch this one in the middle of my tongue. Quinn flashes a satisfied smile.

"Your turn." I pick up one of the berries I missed. She positions herself on her knees and waits for me to throw, but I don't.

"What?"

"Behind you."

She cautiously turns on her knees. "What am I supposed to be looking at?"

"That—that tree."

She follows my gaze. I push off the log from where I've been sitting and crawl up beside her.

"Look."

She parts the bush in front of us to reveal the base of a slender birch tree. Writing is etched onto the side.

Quinn squints. "What does it say?"

It's written sideways with crude, almost illegible, strokes. I tilt my head to the left and sound out the words. "T-H-E . . . T-H-E-Y-'-R-E . . . THEY'RE . . ."

"They're what?"

"THEY'RE C-C-C . . . COMING." Then I say it again, and it sinks in. "They're coming."

CHAPTER 8

Section 2.1 – The Hill is a clandestine operation. Nobody knows about the Hill or the Colony.

QUINN HOOKS MY arm and pulls me into her, rough and protective. My chest heaves.

"Who's coming?"

"I don't know," I say, "but I have a feeling we don't want them to."

She exhales. "That could've been there for a hundred years," she reasons, looking over her shoulder.

I trace the gouges. "Feels fresh."

"Probably a bear. That's what they do. The Manual says they both claw and bite tree bark." She measures the height with her hand. "Not a very big one though."

"First of all, no one's seen a bear in twenty years. I'm pretty sure they're extinct. Secondly, if it was a bear, how in the heck did it learn to spell?"

"I don't know." Quinn shrugs. "Maybe it evolved."

"The Great North American Spelling Bear."

"Alright then, genius, who wrote it?"

I run my finger through the groove of the letter *g*. "Doesn't look like Harlow's writing."

"Wren, it's knifed into a tree."

"I know. And the letters are all uppercase."

"Because if she was being dragged against her will, she'd have time for proper grammar."

"I'm not feeling it."

"Right, *feelings*. Wren, use your head."

"I just think it's old."

"You just said it felt fresh." Quinn takes a step back and then suddenly disappears up to her neck into a hole. We shriek in unison.

She holds onto the earth, elbows splayed as if she's fallen through ice. I have no idea if her feet are dangling in mid-air or if her toes are touching the ground. Her expression suggests the former.

"Hang on," I say, grabbing both wrists.

She groans, legs wriggling.

"Stop moving."

"I don't know deep it is," she says.

I imagine a sinkhole deeper than the ocean, the Mariana Trench, an endless pit, the air filmy and black. "I'll pull you up, just hold on a second." I gradually peel my fingers away from her wrists.

Ember barks frantically, circling the perimeter, most of which is still disguised by tangled vegetation.

"Be careful," Quinn warns, adjusting her position so she can grab onto a tree root. "Don't fall in here with me." Her breaths are shallow and quick.

I need an anchor point. The birch with the writing is

too fine. I don't have any rope, nothing I can use to tie myself to for support. I find her spear wedged at an odd angle between patches of unruly ferns. I yank it free, passing her the blunt end.

"Are you crazy?" she asks.

"Little bit," I mutter, bracing my ankle under the deadfall. "On three, you're going to swing your legs forward. When they kip back, I'm going to pull. Keep the pressure on your elbows and grip the spear as tight as you can."

She replies in hyperventilated breaths. Ember keeps up her hysteric's vigil, pacing and pawing.

"On three," I caution. "Say it with me. One . . . two . . . three."

Her body jerks and swings back expectantly. I angle my torso so I don't get impaled, and I tug with every muscle fiber. Quinn grunts, her pelvis crashing up onto the lip of the crater and I reel her in with a second explosive heave. When I'm satisfied she's safe, I drop the spear and collapse beside her.

Shaking, Quinn rolls onto her back and places a steadying hand on her forehead. "What *was* that?"

"What *is* that," I correct, squeezing her hand. "Natural or man-made?"

"Well, it was concealed, like a trap. I'm guessing someone constructed it."

"Any sense how far down it went?"

"I thought I felt my foot scrape something, but then it was just air."

Ember climbs on top of her and licks her face. Quinn cringes and gently pushes her away.

"Come, Ember."

Quinn stands and tries to find her bearings, her face a flush of sweat.

"Don't ever do that again," I say. "You scared me."

"*You* were scared? Try being the one hanging." She brushes dirt from her clothes. "I'll do my best not to die."

I sidestep around the hole to the other side and peer into the darkness, adjusting my view to take advantage of the fragmented sunlight folding through the trees.

"You see anything?" Quinn asks, drinking.

"Not sure. It seems to curve. I can't tell if I can see the bottom or not."

"Let's keep going." Quinn examines the backs of her arms, twisting her elbows into awkward contortions.

I pull away from the edge, unconvinced I didn't see a glint of something shiny. Water? Metal? The girl with the patch probably shouldn't be the one conducting reconnaissance.

Quinn laces her arms through the straps of her pack.

"You okay?" I ask, gathering my belongings.

She nods. We both glance back at the birch. A wisp of bark curls, levitating in the wind.

"Did Harlow keep a knife?" I ask.

"Dunno. All the girls carry something for protection. Not sure about Mothers. Mine had a claw hammer."

"Dasha had a chisel."

"What, you think your Mother wrote it?"

"No, I'm just saying there are girls with chisels."

"And screwdrivers and jackknifes and pry bars and scrapers."

I sigh. "Right."

"Come on," Quinn urges. "I'm hungry. Besides, we should be more concerned with who *they* are."

She's right. I collect a handful of berries and empty them into my pocket. "But whoever they are, if they *are* coming, we'll kill them."

WE WALK FOR an hour, and Quinn catches her bow on a branch, snapping the string. She alternately grumbles and sighs about it until we approach the edge of a micro-clearing.

"This is good," I say, kicking at the low-slung boughs of a heavy conifer. "We can sleep under here."

Quinn lifts one of the boughs and climbs underneath. "Pass me your pack."

I nudge it with my foot. Ember explores. "Stay close," I call after her, seeing nothing but her blissful waving tail.

Quinn emerges, brushing debris from her knees. She circles the tree. "We should reinforce this side. Bit of a gap back here."

I nod. "Bring your ax?"

"Front pocket." She gestures to her bag. "I gotta pee."

She stumbles over a rock, walks a dozen paces, and disappears behind a thicket of trees.

I kneel and pull her pack towards me. The front zipper snags. When I finally work it open, the ax isn't even there. "Come on, Quinn," I sigh, rifling through the main compartment, pulling out her blanket, and shoving it under the tree. I feel the ax buried at the bottom, the handle smooth. I work it out to the top, knocking the contents out of her bag. A piece of paper sticks to my hand, smelling of sap. I peel it off and flip it over. "What the hell?"

I look for Quinn. She's a good thirty feet away, Ember by her side. I flatten the page against my thigh and study it frantically. It's her page from the Record. *Arrival #151*, and then in smaller print, *Taken*. It continues: *Black skin, born 2086. Temperamental, athletic, emotional.* The "emotional" part has been scribbled over. *Assignment: Hunter.*

"Taken?" I say aloud. What does that even mean? Taken from where? Taken by who? Taken from the Colony to the Hill, I theorize. Like me. Like all of us. But my record mentions nothing of being taken. Do others? I shove the page back into her bag, my heart racing. I could give her the switch for removing it from the Record, but I won't. For now. I watch her stagger back through the brush, Ember bounding beside her, unfazed.

Out of breath, Quinn holds her stomach. "I'm starving."

"Shelter first." I pick up a *Y*-shaped branch. "Grab the other end."

She takes a side, and we fit it over the hole at the base of the tree for a door. Quinn snaps the limb off a dead tree and reinforces an area at the back. Ember sniffs the ground, her fur a matted mess. We don't build a fire. There's no time to build a proper pit or a chimney, nothing to fashion an air pipe from. If we sleep close, it will be warm enough. Daylight's disappearing. I haul a blanket out of my pack and spread it beside Quinn's.

She makes quick work of repairing her bow, takes a haul from the water container, and sits cross-legged across from me. "I can't wait to eat," she says, removing an inner pack of food assembled by the Suppliers. I'm alarmed by the size of the bag; it doesn't look big enough for one meal for a single girl, let alone three days for two. Quinn pulls open the drawstring and flips the brown sack upside down. I hope for venison jerky or snake or dried fish, some type of protein or the savory rye bread one of the Suppliers invented. But the heap of junk that falls out isn't even edible.

"What is this shit?" Quinn hammer-fists the ground. "This isn't food."

"No, it's definitely not." My eyes shift from item to item. "But based on what we do have, I think you took one of the Collector's packs by accident." I finger through the loot. There's an empty glass jar with a lid that leaves an oily residue on my fingers, a few flaps of cardboard, some kind of animal figurine with a chipped ear, a pink stick with bristles, and a large, filthy button-up shirt covered in palm trees. I spread out the shirt and can't get over the size of it, nor can I imagine anyone fitting into it. It smells like a swamp.

Quinn punches the trunk of the tree, then immediately bites her good hand to silence her agony.

"What did you do *that* for?"

"We have no food!"

"Yeah, well, now we have no food and no way to get any. I brought you along so you could hunt. How are you going to do that?" I take her wrist and examine her hand. The skin has been torn clean off two of her knuckles, and the blood is flecked with bark. I pour water over the area, and it trickles down her forearm like a tiny, bloodstained waterfall. I tear a strip of cloth from the shirt we've been using to mark our route and wrap it around her hand. She winces in pain, her teeth still clenched around her good hand. Ember paces, whimpering.

I didn't bring any meds. *Why didn't I bring any medicine?* Who ventures into the Eastside Forest without a single herb? "Did you bring any arnica salve? Cow parsnip? Devil's club?"

Quinn uses her foot to draw her pack towards her, protecting it with her leg. She shakes her head.

I part the tree branch and survey what's nearby. "We could always try a few puffballs in the morning."

"Mushrooms don't do anything to stop swelling," Quinn mutters.

"Do they stop bad tempers?"

Quinn scowls, her eyes teary. I pull lunch leftovers from my pack, which consist of a sizeable chunk of bread and a smaller piece I took from Arrow.

"Thank you." Her voice trembles as she chooses the larger of the two pieces. She eats lying on her side, both knees tucked up under her chest with her head on my lap, personifying the shape of the island. Her bandaged hand balances on her pack. She whispers, "Sorry," and closes her eyes.

I sit, conflicted, hungry, and exhausted, my back against the tree, the weight of Quinn's head pressing down so hard on my thigh that it pulls uncomfortably on my hip. Her mass of hair spills out on either side of my leg, and I remove a few bits that are entangled in her curls. She would never do this back at the Hill. It's usually Smalls who crawl onto my lap and seek comfort, not giant teenagers. Even when we do share a bed, we almost always sleep back to back, our spines lined up like firewood, tools in a tray.

I think of the older girls who pair off, the ones who hold hands and kiss at night, their breath heavy, bodies moving and cheeks flushed—all of our cheeks flushed, ears pricked and backs turned. I kiss my fingertip and place it on Quinn's mouth.

I roll the palm tree shirt into a bundle, place it beside me, and then transfer Quinn's head onto it. I do the same with one of my own shirts. I feel within my pants for the drawing of the figure I took from the Record and try to find a comfortable position to sleep in. Once I'm settled, I remove the drawing from my pocket and study it. Definitely looks like a boy, though there's nothing about this particular drawing to suggest he's "violent" or, as Section 8.1 of the Manual indicates, that he might "abuse his power to control, oppress, or dominate." Other than the size of his back, he looks almost benign. He could be a goat. "Right, Ember?"

The dog bows, circles, and paws at the ground before settling. I pet her side, hold the paper close, and contemplate every shaded line, hoping there might be more to the picture. But in the blink of an eye, the image is rendered invisible by the blackness of night. Erased.

The realization that I'm so far from the Hill sends shockwaves of panic through my core, like swimming underwater and coming up for air, only to learn that a riptide has carried you out to sea. I move closer to Quinn, chest to chest. Tears saturate my patch, and I fall asleep like her: vulnerable, scared, and starving.

CHAPTER 9

`Section 8.3 - ... eliminate him.`

THE NEXT MORNING, light leaks though the branches and casts a strange pattern on Quinn's cheek, like a snowflake, rare and spectacular. My stomach growls before I have time to stretch. The woods are eerily silent. I crawl to the makeshift door and remove the shielding branches. There are mushrooms on the ground, but before I have a chance to pick them, something grabs my ankle, and I unleash an ear-splitting shriek into the forest.

I shake myself free and find Quinn in hysterics behind me.

"You idiot!"

"Hey! It was just a joke."

"Well, it wasn't funny."

"You're in a mood."

"Can you blame me? You took up all the space. I slept on a root."

Quinn shrugs and hoists herself off the ground. "What's the plan?" she asks over a yawn.

I fiddle for the compass in my pocket and hold it up to a beam of sunlight. The needle fluctuates. "I think we should keep heading east."

"Until . . ."

"Until we find something. Like a cove or a bay. If someone took Harlow, they probably didn't stick around. There's got to be an exit point."

"We're on an island," Quinn says, carefully unwrapping the cloth on her damaged hand. "Everything is an exit point."

"I'm sure they didn't jump off a cliff."

"You don't know that. Maybe there was a raft waiting for them down below."

"Shaped like a unicorn with a place to put their drinks. Remember that? Brand new in the box."

"Seats ten!"

I smile.

"She could have been airlifted."

"By who? The Colony doesn't do airlifts. When's the last time you saw a helicopter over here?"

Quinn winces at the sight of her knuckles, bloody and swollen. "At least three months ago. Maybe four."

"Exactly. And judging by the terrain, I don't see anywhere for a helicopter to land." I yank a fiddlehead from the ground and pass it to Quinn. "Eat."

She brushes dirt from the coiled top and takes a bite. I pick a dozen stalks, make quick work of one, and toss the remainder into my pack. Quinn stretches, claps her hands as if summoning herself to get to work, and begins dismantling the shelter. Ember hunches over a rock, nose to the ground. Probably eating something dead.

I whistle. "Come on, girl."

She continues to chew until I whistle again. She disappears behind some trees and emerges, pleased. A game.

I tear a strip of fabric from the palm tree shirt with my knife, press some lichen into Quinn's wounds, and re-wrap her hand. She is quiet from start to finish. When the knot is tied, she examines her fingers and nods approvingly.

I slip my pack on over my shoulders. Quinn manages to do the same without help. "What are you going to do with your spear?"

She scoops it up with her left hand as if there was never any doubt. "Should we check in with the girls?"

I wonder the same, conflicted. Surely, they'd radio if there were an issue. "It's still early. Let's get a couple of hours in and then try. I told Clover to use it only in case of emergency. I don't want to alarm her."

Quinn nods. I check the compass, and we head out. The first hour is treacherous, as we navigate deadfall and steep terrain. I slash my cheek and the back of my arms on thorns sharp as fingernails. Quinn takes a perceived shortcut and nearly twists an ankle. We break at the foot of a cliff, exhausted, demoralized. At any other time, it would be an easy scale. Now it seems insurmountable.

"What do you say? Quick break and then we go for it?"

Quinn tips her canteen back and drinks long and hard. "You know," she starts, breathing heavy, "we've been out here almost twenty-four hours, and nothing's happened to us."

"Yet."

Quinn raises her eyebrows.

"What's that supposed to mean?" I ask, sizing the rock wall.

"It's just . . ." she pauses and looks behind her, as if to make sure no one's listening. "It just doesn't seem *that* dangerous out here."

"You fell in a hole."

"Besides that."

"Besides that? You almost died."

"I did not," she argues. "And I've come to the conclusion that it was more natural than manufactured."

"Is that what you're telling yourself?"

"Forests have sinkholes. It's in the Manual."

"I've never seen that written anywhere." I try to excavate my memory. "Name the section."

"6.3 or 7.3? One of them. CRATERS, HOLES, AND CREVICES."

"Fine," I relent. "But I betcha it says nothing about finding them near trees with warnings etched into their sides."

"What are you implying, Wren?"

"I get the desire to believe that the hole was simply part of the landscape, no more bizarre than frozen methane bubbles or polar lights. But regardless of how it got there, we are still very much in danger. We were on the Hill, and even more so off it."

A fresh wave of fear ripples through my body. I check behind me. Quinn pulls a shirt over her head, pretending not to listen. A sulky protest.

"We haven't reached the limestone. There are definitely animals that could hurt us out here," I say, kicking at a pile of coyote scat, "and you yourself saw a boy closer to the Hill than we are now."

Quinn sighs.

"Never mind the fact that someone dragged Harlow into the woods."

"Okay, yes. Shut up already. You're right." She shakes her head. "I guess . . . it just doesn't seem so bad. We're not dead."

"True. We are very much alive. Right, Ember?"

The dog nuzzles my side.

"Because I thought we might have died already," Quinn says. "Instantly."

"A testament to our training."

"Or maybe the Colony got it wrong."

I gulp quietly and don't reply. The thought bounces around my brain, a bee in a jar. I change the subject. "You ready to climb that?" I gesture at the cliff looming before us.

"I'm always ready," she says, pressing her hip against the base and sinking into a lunge. "But you first." She motions to her leg. "Hop on."

I drop my pack and carefully position my foot on her

thigh, searching overhead for a ledge to grip. I count to three in my head and hoist myself up. Quinn grunts under my weight and then exhales.

"You got it?" she asks.

"Almost," I wheeze, pulling straight up, finding a foothold. I drag myself over the lip, gouging my stomach. I'm more tired and hungry than I thought, the climb leaving me dizzy and a little stunned. I regroup, encouraged by the sight of a blueberry bush.

"You ready?" I call down over the edge.

Quinn nods and tosses our packs up one at a time, followed by her spear.

"Where's Ember?"

"She took off that way," she gestures, "trying to follow you."

I lie on my stomach and reach down over the side. "Take my wrist."

With only one useable hand, Quinn falters on her first few attempts, but eventually finds her footing and makes it over the top. She lands in a heap, beat, and doesn't attempt to stand. I step over her and look out. Twenty meters down is a clearing.

"Quinn," I say, bending to shake her shoulder. "I see a clearing. A huge one."

She lifts her head, straining her neck in the direction I'm facing. "So?"

"So? Maybe there's something there. A helicopter, food, Harlow."

"If there's a helicopter down there you'd be able to see it, genius. Unless they too have evolved and now fly invisibly."

"Ha ha." I conceal a smile. I'm about to haul my pack up from the ground when I catch something out of the corner of my eye—movement at the edge of the clearing.

I shrink to my knees. Right now, I stand out like a flag on a pole, begging for someone, something, to see me. "Shit."

"What?" Quinn groans, wiping away sweat from her face.

"N-nothing."

"Not nothing," she says, alarmed. "What is it?"

"I thought I saw something."

Quinn rises to her elbows and drags herself behind the cover of the blueberry bush spilling from a rock crevice. "Where?"

I drop to my stomach beside her. "To the left. Near those poplars."

"I don't see anything." Quinn cautiously raises and lowers her head.

"There's no reason for anyone to be out here, right?"

"Right," she agrees, lifting her torso for a second scan of the clearing below. "I don't see anyone. I think we're good."

Ember stands from where she was curled behind us, feverishly licking her paw.

"Sit down, girl," I whisper. "Sit."

Ember wags her tail.

"Come on, you stupid whore," Quinn says. "Sit *down*." She turns to face me. "That dog is dumber than a hockey skate."

"She's not."

We wait a few minutes, faces pressed against the rock, when Quinn props herself up. "I think we're good now. Let's keep going."

I sit up, a new ache in my shoulder, and study the landscape. A pair of crows squawk and dart frenetically between the trees. There's nothing else, except for the faint trickle of a distant stream. I withdraw the radio from my pack and switch the dial to *on*. It crackles to life. "Wren to Clover. You there?"

"You didn't say 'over,'" Quinn says.

"Whatever. It's not going to stop her from replying."

"Section 7.4 of the Manual. TWO-WAY RADIO ETIQUETTE. *'Identify yourself, the recipient of the message, and then say* over *to indicate that you've finished speaking.'*"

"You're getting on my nerves," I say, shoving her arm.

"Only 'cause I love you." She sticks her tongue out childishly and jabs me back.

"This is Wren to Clover," I repeat. "Clover, are you there, OVER."

Quinn smiles. "You know that rhymed."

I roll my eyes. Muffled feedback buzzes from the speaker. We instinctively lean in to see if we can make anything out.

"Wren to Clover," I repeat.

"Over," Quinn adds, pulling the radio toward her and pressing it against her ear.

We hold our breath. There's a muffled crackle, and then a voice rings out—loud, clear, and distinctly not female.

Except it's not projecting from the radio. A boy steps out from behind the trees.

"Draco!" he hollers.

Quinn and I drop back to the ground, my head glancing off a rock.

I whisper, "What the hell does that mean?"

Quinn gestures toward Ember, who stands on the edge of the cliff, facing the clearing with pricked ears. Her tail wags eagerly.

"Draco!" The boy in the clearing calls again, kicking at the ground, defeated. "Come here, boy."

"*Boy?*" I hiss.

Ember starts barking.

"Ember," I whisper through clenched teeth. "Quit it."

But Ember doesn't. She paces the cliff edge, searching for a way down and pawing the rock, and resumes barking.

I lift my head enough to see the boy look up. "Draco!" This time, his voice is victorious, elated. Perhaps even a bit pathetic.

"Oh my God," I whisper. "Ember's a boy."

"Get down," Quinn snarls, her pupils dilated. "The actual boy can probably see you."

I lift up an inch and shift my body to the right, where a tree has grown from a crack. I'm lucky if it conceals half of me. At the same time, Ember—Draco—scampers down the rock from the side we climbed up, underbrush cracking under her paws, the occasional whimper when she—he—gets held up by an obstacle.

I cover my mouth to stop my breathing, which I'm

83

sure is the volume of ten girls hauling a boat uphill for repairs. Quinn looks over. Her face is buried in her shirt.

"Wren?" A crackle. "Wren, this is Blue, over."

I wave frantically at Quinn. *Turn it off*, I mouth.

She fumbles with her bad hand and drops the radio. The message continues. ". . . smoke signal . . ." There's a screech of interference, silence, and then Blue's voice—or Clover returns. All we can make out is, "No babies." Quinn rights the two-way radio and switches it off.

"Who's there?" The boy's voice is closer than before, as if he's right below us. Draco barks.

"We know you're up there." Another voice.

Quinn and I stare at each other, our eyes swelling with fear. I can see her heart beating in her chest, like it might erupt.

What do we do? she mouths.

I glare back at her uselessly, paralyzed. I've got nothing but a pocketknife. Quinn's bow and arrows are strewn around her feet, and even if I had some way to reach them, I'm a terrible shot. Once I tried to shoot a gull and almost took out a Small.

I close my eyes and try to recall the Manual. Section 8.1 . . . *A boy might abuse his power to control, oppress, or dominate.* No, 8.3. *If you encounter a boy, take swift and violent action to eliminate him.* How the heck do I do that from up here? I rack the library of my brain for Section 9, DEFENSE. *Killing with a crossbow, knife combat, using a spear to kill an attacker, jiu-jitsu methods and submissions.* How are any of those

84

helpful right now? I look down at my fluttering hands, willing them to stop.

I make eye contact with Quinn, but her focus is beyond me. "Quinn," I whisper, making a stabbing gesture.

"We can easily get to you," a boy taunts from below.

Is that a third voice? How many of them *are* there? I hold my stomach, as if to steady the nausea now swirling through my body like poison. I'm terrified. Before I have time to process, though, Quinn is next to me, standing.

I look up at her. "What are you doing?"

Her injured hand trembles, hovering over my head.

"I'll kill you," she spits down at the boys.

Feeling ridiculous, I scramble to my feet, withdrawing my knife from my pocket and take a position beside Quinn. There are three boys below, a good five stories down. The boy in the middle—the one I first saw enter the clearing—is bigger than the other two, intimidating even from my vantage point. His hair hangs to his chin. He throws up his arms and has the wingspan of a bear. Ember circles in front of him.

The way she used to circle around me.

"We're not going to hurt you," he says. His voice is low, as if he's underground.

"Well, we're going to kill you," Quinn shouts.

The other boys laugh. One is fair and about my height, with unruly hair the color of a birch tree, ears for days. He holds a crossbow—lazily, for now. A kill, likely fresh, is slung across the other boy's shoulders. A deer. His body language suggests he feels more inconvenienced than threatened.

"What, are you gonna kill us with that spear you can barely hold up?" the blond one says.

The spear wavers in Quinn's left hand. We both see it.

"My good arm's injured," she counters.

"Quinn," I sneer. "You don't tell the enemy your weaknesses."

"He was making fun of me."

"Yeah, well, which arm do you think he's going to attack?"

"At least I did something. You stayed on the ground, oh-fearless-Head-Girl."

My cheeks flare up and my jaw tenses, sending shockwaves through my skull.

"Leave now, and no one gets hurt." I wave my knife, the light glinting off the blade.

Quinn draws back her spear. The blond boy places an arrow in his bow.

"Whoa, whoa, whoa." The boy in the middle makes a *stop* gesture with his hands. "No one's going to hurt anyone."

"Section 8.6," Quinn recites. "Never trust a boy."

The hunter slides the deer off his back and dumps it on the ground. "What's she talking about?"

The middle boy shakes his head. "Ignore it," he says. "They're from the Hill. They don't know."

Quinn shoots me a look and nearly drops her spear. "How does he know about the Hill?"

My mouth is so dry, it feels like it's been wiped with a blanket. My head rings. "No idea."

The next thing I know, Quinn is roaring, mouth agape, eyes small and focused. She hurls the spear over the side of the cliff. I look away and then quickly rush to the edge to see if she's hit anyone.

"Nice one," the hunter says sarcastically. "But she was already dead."

The spear bounces slightly, suspended from the backside of the doe.

"That was a terrible shot," I say.

The blond boy draws back on the bowstring.

I drop my knife and throw up my hands. "Don't shoot."

"What are you doing?" Quinn paces beside me.

"Do you see any other options right now?"

She concedes, slowly lifting her arms over her head.

The blond boy doesn't let up on his crossbow.

"Can you just leave now? Pretend you never saw us?" I tug at the collar of my shirt like it might create more space to breathe. What if the Colony finds out? What will they do to Quinn? What will they do to me?

CHAPTER 10

Section 8.2 – Boys and men are enemies of the Hill. Do not believe their lies.

THE BOY IN the middle nods and begins to retreat.

"Come on," the blond says, kicking the ground, disappointed. The other crosses his arms. That's it? That's all it took? I exhale, almost laugh, and almost vomit. Quinn drops her arms to her sides heavily. Tears form in her eyes.

Then the boy stops and turns around.

"Are you, uh, by any chance lost?"

Quinn and I yell *yes* and *no* simultaneously.

The hunter shakes his head, pulls Quinn's spear out of the deer, and tosses it aimlessly to the side.

"I want to punch him in the throat," Quinn mutters.

"We're fine," I correct, though the pitch of my voice suggests otherwise. I hold my throat. Again, the trio turns and heads across the clearing. And then I look at the deer, small and lifeless—a juvenile—and I remember Harlow. "Wait," I shout. The hunter and the blond boy don't stop. Only the tall one does. He looks up, shielding his eyes from the sun.

"Did you see a girl? About this big?" I measure to my chest. "She might've come this way?"

He shakes his head. "There's no one here."

"We know *that's* not true," Quinn says, cocking her eyebrow.

"I think we should talk to him." I lower my pack over the cliff's edge, dropping it when I can't reach any farther.

"This is nuts." Quinn's lips are pinched, but her eyes are all for it. She peers over the side, walks about ten feet into a clump of trees, and then says, "I think we can get down over here."

I maneuver my way through the tangle of roots, careful not to get swatted in the face by a rogue branch. The descent is steep, punishing our knees. When it's easy enough to jump, we do so without hesitation.

The boy waits, tousling Draco's head and patting his back affectionately. His smile is animated. I watch.

"What?" Quinn asks. "Why are you staring at him like that?"

"Ember."

"Draco."

"Whatever." I wave a hand. "He loves that dog. Like I did."

Quinn takes a few cautious steps forward. "You still have your knife?"

"Of course." I feel my front pocket. "Snatched it up when they started to leave."

"Good."

Six feet away from him, I lose my confidence. I may come up to his chest if I'm on my tiptoes. His shoulders are as wide as the Shed. Like anything worthy of fear, he is both majestic and horrific. A scream forms in my gut. My eyes blur.

One of the other boys shouts, "Roman, hurry up."

He waves him off. "Thank you for looking after my dog."

"Are you going to abuse your power?" Quinn asks, fists clenched.

"What?"

"Are you going to try to control us?" I ask.

"No."

"How about oppress, dominate, or rape us?"

"No!" Roman shifts uncomfortably, his face flushed red. "What are you talking about?"

"How do you know about the Hill?" Quinn presses.

The blond boy starts walking back. The hunter also stops, but sits on what looks like an old stone wall. Ruins. He massages his shoulders and takes a drink from a canteen.

"Everyone knows about the Hill," Roman replies.

My heart thrashes inside my rib cage. I can't believe I'm standing this close to a boy. Two of them. They're definitely strong, muscles carved and contracted, but they don't look particularly dangerous. Not when you look in their eyes. "What does that mean, exactly?" I ask. "Who's *everyone*?"

Roman takes a step forward. I pull my knife out of my pocket.

"Whoa," he says. "Would you put that thing down?"

"Get back."

He obliges with a sigh. I lower my knife.

"*Everyone* refers to the people in our village."

Quinn makes a sweeping gesture from one side of the clearing to the other. "Is this your village?"

The blond boy snickers.

I point my knife at him. "What is your name?"

"Finn," Roman answers for him. "And no, this isn't a village. A village is a place where people live together in a kind of permanent settlement."

"YOU LIVE ON THE ISLAND?" Quinn bellows.

Both boys shudder at the shrillness of her voice.

"On the North end. We've always been there."

The map. The blackened head. The symbol. The symbol was a flag marking the village. I elbow Quinn but say nothing. This is why the map is blacked out. The Colony didn't want us to know. Why would they keep that a secret?

I swallow hard. It feels like the forest is on fire.

"Then why are you all the way down here?" I visualize the map, noting how far south we are.

"He lost his dumb dog," Finn replies.

"See?" Quinn whispers. "It's not just me. Dog's an idiot."

"She's a great dog." Grief hangs on my shoulders, like a Small climbing my back.

Roman looks at me. We lock eyes, as if there's a band of energy between us. I don't know what it is.

Quinn shoves me.

"I've been combing this place for a month, looking for him," Roman says, giving Draco a reassuring squeeze.

"Well, Wren here's been playing house with him."

I fire her a salty look.

"What?" she says. "It's true."

"Why do you wear a patch?" Finn asks.

The hunter approaches, seemingly feeling left out. He has a scar on his left cheek. Half of his ear is missing. I try not to stare. We're now outnumbered.

"Can't see out of this eye."

"So how come you two are out here and not back on your garbage dump?"

"Garbage dump?" Quinn raises her eyebrows.

"Trash Mountain, the Great Bear Landfill, the old dump—whatever you want to call it."

"The Hill," Roman says quietly.

Quinn and I stand there frozen, speechless. I try to tell her telepathically to say something.

"Landfill," she begins. "What's a . . ."

"We get it," I interrupt. "We live on a garbage dump." Do we? Is that what it is? I nudge Quinn.

"A *reclaimed* garbage dump," Roman offers apologetically.

"Still a dump," the hunter adds.

"And still disgusting," Finn says.

"The Hill provides us with everything we need to survive." I sound pathetic. Does it? Of course it does. We have fresh water and tools and three-legged chairs and broken glass and hockey skates!

And a Manual of lies.

"So does our village, and we don't have to dig it up." The hunter holds up an apple, ripe and perfectly round.

"Then maybe we'll take your village," Quinn snarls.

The boys exchange incredulous glances and laugh. I don't react, instead counting in my head, the way my Mother taught me. I focus on the sun warming my cheek and try to imagine eating the hunter's glowing red apple when Quinn swings at Finn with a left hook. Her fist grazes his cheek.

Roman steps in to defend Finn, but I get in the way. I drag his arm, and when he resists, I take him down—single leg, flat on his back, just like in training. I'm on top of him, heavy. His breath smells like smoke. We lock eyes. His are the shade of a garter snake.

And then his hands are on my chest, and he pushes me off him. I scramble to get up, adrenaline coursing through me, but he trips me with a sweep of his foot. We tussle. My patch twists, the elastic pinching my cheek and ruffling my eyelid. I try to take his back. I slide my arm around his neck and attempt a choke, spitting a piece of his hair from my mouth. He escapes, gets side mount, and then he takes my arm. Draco barks and bounds wildly in my periphery.

Panic.

Beside me, Quinn and Finn exchange shots. Both are bloodied and staggering. I try to pull my arm away, but the hunter hovers over us. Roman tugs harder, my elbow cranked toward the sky, which has the blue hue of winter. My arm is going to snap.

I taste grass; I taste rock. I taste the quasi-sweet rank of boy, like a root, dirty and edible. Then I tap.

He lets go, and I roll onto my side, cradling my arm.

"Now what?" the hunter asks, echoing what we're all thinking.

Quinn spits out a tooth. Finn's right eye is the size of a fist and poised to swell shut.

Roman brushes debris from his pants. His shirt is ripped, hanging open like a door. "Jiujitsu," he says, breath still catching. "Where'd you learn to fight like that?"

"The Manual," I mutter, trying to stand.

He offers a hand, which I bat away.

Finn wipes a line of snot from his face. "You guys are bloody wild."

"Girls," Quinn corrects.

"Animals," offers the hunter, shaking his head in dismay. "But I give you credit. That's the most entertainment I've had in weeks."

I catch Roman staring at me. "What?" I ask, testing my arm's range of motion, the back of my head pulsing.

"Why'd you *do* that?" he asks, attempting to piece together his shirt.

I'm torn between apologizing and stabbing him. Draco prances over and licks my hand, like he's delivering a peace offering. We watch, part mesmerized, part exhausted.

"Sorry," Roman says. "We didn't mean to scare you."

"She hit me first!" Finn says. A button dangles from his shirt collar by a thread.

"Let's go." The hunter gestures to the deer slung across the ruins like a sacrificial offering. "Before something picks up her scent."

"Like a bear?" Quinn asks.

"Possible, but not likely. Probably a cougar, coyote, wolf."

Quinn jabs me with her elbow. "Told you there's still bears around here."

"Yeah, I get that," I snap back. "They just don't write on trees."

"I'm not even going to ask." The hunter turns, waving without looking. Finn follows behind.

"Don't forget your spear." The hunter kicks at a spot where the grass is thick. Quinn rises on her tiptoes and then limps off to retrieve it.

"What?" I gather my scattered belongings and stuff them into my pack.

"Nothing," Roman says. He picks up the bristled pink stick from the Collector's bag. "Your toothbrush?"

"My what?"

"Your toothbrush."

I shake my head. He seems confused. The radio is facedown, bending the stalk of an incredibly hearty weed.

"Wren to Clover, are you there? Over." Why was there a smoke signal and no babies?

"Do you need anything before I go?" Roman asks.

"I don't need your help. I have to get back to the Hill."

Quinn rubs the tip of her spear with her shirt. I

gather my hair on top of my head, re-tying the elastic. My stomach growls.

Roman raises his eyebrows. "You hungry?"

I fiddle with the radio.

"Here," he says, pulling something from a satchel tied around his waist.

"What is it?"

"Bannock." He holds it up to the light. "At least, it was until you landed on top of it."

I take it and eat it savagely, nearly choking.

"Whoa." He smiles. "You can fight, and you can eat."

"So?" I brush by him and head toward Quinn.

"Colony," he says.

I feel him reading the back of my neck. Fear hangs on my shoulders like a heavy hand. My heart skips. Ahead, Quinn forages in a thicket of bushes growing alongside the ruins. I face him. He's pensive, pale.

"They'll want to know," he says.

"They'll want to know what?"

"That I saw you. Off the Hill. That one of you is missing."

"Please," I beg, unable to not sound desperate, my voice diving. We'd both be banished, probably separated. I may never see her again. I grab his arm. "Don't tell them." He can tell them? I scan his body for some sign of a radio, a pocket flare, a megaphone like the one we found on the Hill, red and obnoxious. Nothing. He has to be lying. *Never trust a boy.*

He wrestles away. "You're not very nice."

Finn and the hunter disappear into the woods on the other side of the clearing.

"I have to get back to the Hill." I stare up at the cliff Quinn and I scaled down earlier, analyzing how we might get back up now that we're both broken. Quinn looks like something we might dig up on the Hill, bent and bloodied, manically eating hooker berries.

"You know there's a shortcut. Back to the Hill."

I cock an eye, suspicious.

"Follow the cliffs. Go south a couple hundred paces toward the old cell tower. Just watch the rocks."

"Limestone Pass."

"Yes."

"*Where one can't go barefoot.*"

"Well—" Roman starts.

"The rocks will slice your feet up. The Manual says they're more lethal than an ax blade. That a single misstep can sever the skin, resulting in extreme blood loss and certain . . ." My voice trails off when Roman smiles, as if I've told him something amusing. The way I look at Arrow when she says she wants to be assigned to the hummingbirds.

"Your friends left a long time ago," Quinn says, sidling up beside me, the gap in her mouth from the missing tooth larger than I expected, almost ghoulish.

Roman nods and turns his gaze toward me. "The rocks—they're no more dangerous than any other around here. They're the least of your worries."

"What's that supposed to mean?"

Roman looks out over the clearing as if he's heard

something in the distance, while Draco noses around the ground, seeking something suitable to roll in.

"Well?" Quinn asks.

"Rumor has it, the Mainland's low on girls." He summons Draco with a sharp whistle.

"What does that mean?" I demand.

"The girls. They keep disappearing."

"Disappearing?"

"You know. Taken."

Taken. I look at Quinn, but she's distracted, touching her jaw as if checking to see whether it's still in place.

"We should head back," I mumble.

"Be careful," Roman warns.

"We're always careful."

He nods, unconvinced, and turns to go. After a few paces, he breaks into a run. He doesn't look back. Only Draco pauses before they disappear, swallowed by the forest, where the secrets hide.

CHAPTER 11

Section 4.4 - Black smoke signals the arrival of babies. Blue smoke signals the delivery of supplies.

I FIND QUINN collapsed in a pile on the ground. "What just happened?"

I stare at my trembling hands, as if the answer lies in their movement. "I don't know." I kneel beside her, weak as a hatchling, my face damp with sweat.

"My lip hurts."

"So does my elbow."

"I can't really see out of this eye." She points.

I straighten my patch. "That makes two of us."

She touches her jaw again, opening and closing her mouth.

"They knew about us," I say. "They know about the Colony."

Quinn spits on her hand. "Don't know if I believe that."

"What don't you believe? They knew that we lived on a garbage dump."

"*Reclaimed* garbage dump," Quinn mockingly corrects. "If they live on the island, they'd probably know about the dump. Doesn't mean they know we *live* on it."

"Quinn, he referred to it by name. He actually said the Hill."

"Of course he did. It's a bloody hill. What else would he call it?" She tries to tie her shoelace with one hand and fails.

I crouch to help, unsure if I'll be able to stand back up. My muscles are fish-like. "It was more than that," I say, re-lacing her boot. "It was almost like they had a relationship with them. The Colony."

Quinn tugs the tongue of her other boot. Her knuckles are speckled with blood and bits of landscape.

"He told me the Colony would want to know that he saw us. That Harlow was missing. "

"You have any water?"

I hand her my canteen. "Did you hear what I said?"

Quinn nearly empties it in a single pour. "Yes." She wipes a drip from her chin. "You think we should go after them?"

"I asked him not to tell."

"That's helpful. The Hill has been saved."

I don't admit that Roman gave me food. "You have a better suggestion?"

"Slit their throats."

That he offered help. "Why would they be working with the Colony? You think they could be?"

"More like why would the Colony be working with them? They're *boys*."

"That's my point."

The sun gets hot, sudden and intense. We both freeze to tilt our heads upward, drawn to its primitive powers. As though its rays might heal and advise us both.

"If we head this way, there's a shortcut back to the Hill."

"That's the opposite way from where we came," Quinn protests.

"It'll take us to the beach."

"We can't go through Limestone Pass."

"They're just rocks."

"You know this boy for all of five minutes, and you trust his directions?"

I scan the forest; amid the dizzying array of near-black spindles, every tree looks identical. "Look, they seem to know this place. And we have to get back. I can't get a hold of Clover. We still have no idea why there was a smoke signal and why there were no babies."

"It's not unusual for the Colony to send a few supply boats, especially after a Departure Ceremony. And it's about time they did. We're low on everything. They didn't even send anything with the last Arrivals."

"Then the smoke signal would have been blue. It sounded like they were expecting babies. They must have seen black smoke." I pause. "Beck said we shouldn't expect babies for at least a year."

"Babies come all the time."

"Not twice in the same week."

"So someone shot off smoke in the wrong color. Or maybe the babies were just late. The boats could've gotten caught in a current. Why do you think you can't get a hold of anyone on the Hill? Because they're likely on the beach this very minute, doling out names and wiping away tears. You should be relieved we don't have to listen to it."

"I love naming the babies."

"Fine, but there's nothing to love about all the screaming and crying." Quinn mock-plugs her ears.

"I never cried when I came."

"Because you were almost five."

I shrug. Sometimes I get flashes of my life before the Hill. I don't share them with anyone, these abbreviated fragments. A room with walls as thick as an elk's neck, a round window in the corner, a bed off the ground. Sometimes I can close my eyes and still feel my feet dangling. I remember the weightless joy of being carried, my head on a shoulder, bony and secure. Letting go of someone's hand, the same size as mine. The rhythmic rocking of waves, screeching gulls, a row of babies bundled at my feet. The beach. The girl with the magnificent hair who helped me off the boat.

I head in the direction of the shortcut. If I understand Roman's directions correctly, it'll shave a half-day off the return trip. Quinn follows, as I knew she would.

"That was quite the takedown," she says, catching up. "He went down pretty hard."

"We both did." I haul up the back of my shirt to show off a mark I can't see but know is there.

"Ouch," Quinn says, running her finger along its perimeter. "Still. Nice technique." She puts her arm around me, and we walk like this through the clearing until it's obvious the position hurts her shoulder. She pulls her arm away, wincing, just in time for a fortress of trees to replace the open meadow. Immediately, a branch snaps in her face.

"Sorry," I say, stumbling over some deadfall.

"What's another scratch," she replies, pointing to her face.

There are so many lines that her face reminds me of the bear tree. The next hour is a grueling scramble, the forest floor three feet deep, tangled with plants. We barely speak, all of our energy pouring into our legs.

"Some shortcut," Quinn musters, dragging herself onto a rock.

I take an alternate route through a hoard of skunk cabbage. "Finally!" I cry. "A game trail."

Quinn stands and smiles for the first time in a thousand steps.

"And that"—I point—"must be the old cell tower."

We stare at the structure, the crisscross of metal narrowing toward the sky, the antenna like the tines of a fork. The Manual makes short mention of these, only stating their existence. You can see another from the top of the Hill, poking out from the north.

Quinn rises on her toes. "I can see the ocean," she says.

"Then we're going the right way."

Lingonberries the color of flushed cheeks grow trailside, and we eat what we pick. They are tart uncooked, but we need the calories. We refill our canteens from a stream, the water so filtered from the rocks that we don't need to boil it.

The forest begins to thin as the tower nears, and the landscape eventually transitions to rock. Limestone Pass. We are cautious at first as we navigate the cracks, minding a fissure wider than my forearm, but as Roman suggested, there's nothing extraordinary about these rocks. Not like the Manual says. Why?

I'm beginning to think I can write a manual on inaccuracies in the Manual.

"Scat," I tell Quinn, my boot nudged up against a mass.

"What kind?" She kneels, examining the pile from all angles. "Badger."

"Not fox?" I sigh, turning three hundred and sixty degrees. "We'll need fire tonight."

"It's not fresh," she says, "if that helps."

We stop at the foot of the tower. Quinn reaches up and traces a metal beam. "Think you can climb it?"

"Why me?"

She holds up her battered hand. "Better view up there than down here. See if you can find the Hill."

A rusted sign dangles from a single bolt. *No climbing.* "Give me a boost."

Quinn bends lazily. "I can't go any lower," she groans.

I kneel on her back and then hoist myself up until I reach a ladder suspended from a crossbeam. A few rungs in, Quinn walks back toward the woods.

"Where are you going?"

"Pee," she hollers.

"Don't get lost."

"You'll be able to see me," she calls. "Not that I want you to watch . . ." Her voice trails off. "Don't fall."

Don't fall. My body feels heavier with each pull. I stop at a juncture of beams and look out toward the ocean, gray and indefinite. Seabirds populate the sky, rising and swooping through wisps of cloud. I climb higher, my feet navigating the thinning rails with less certainty. Halfway up the tower, the ladder stops. Sawed off. I turn cautiously, pressing my back to the metal, balancing on my heels to face north.

The Hill's shoulder, bony and square, shows off in the distance. But the details are flimsy, a sand picture blurred by a wave. The Hill looks both close enough to touch and as distant as a star.

My eyes get lost in the zigzag of trees. I can only approximate the beach. A faint pillar of black smoke curls offshore. Is it a boat? No. I stick out my neck for a better view, but a wall of fog moves in, a ghost ship coloring everything, dull and thick.

I turn back to face the metal, my shirt snagging on a bent spike, my bare skin flush against a rail. I descend in long clumsy steps. Out of my periphery, I follow Quinn snaking from the woods back onto the rocks.

"You gotta jump," she says, standing under me. Her voice wavers.

"What's wrong?"

"Nothing," she spits, crossing one leg over the other.

"It's too high."

"Then swing down."

"With one arm?"

An overexaggerated sigh. She stands directly underneath the ladder and taps her shoulder. "Put your foot here, then jump."

I position my foot and half-jump, half-fall from the tower, landing in a heap. Before I even get back to my feet, Quinn's already wrestled her pack over her shoulders.

"What?" she says. "Let's go."

She turns toward the shore, passing under the tower and straddling a crevasse. There's a spot on the back of her pants, dark and damp. Blood.

"You got your cycle." I scramble behind her.

"No." She doesn't turn around.

"It's no big deal, Quinn, everyone gets it. It's completely normal."

She whips around to face me, curls striking my cheek. "What are you, the Manual?"

I flinch.

"I don't *want* the cycle!" she yells.

"No one *wants* it," I argue, "but it's nothing to worry about. Completely natural." I try not to look down. "Did you at least find some moss?"

"Yes."

"Then what's your problem?"

"I don't want Smalls."

"Why would you get a Small? Your Assignment is Hunter. No one would ever reassign you, and if they did, they certainly wouldn't make you a Mother."

"Do you know why we have cycles?"

"The cycle . . ." My thought trickles. "The cycle . . ."

"Section 7.3," Quinn recites. *"The cycle is a repetitive occurrence that enables a girl's body to produce a Small."*

I laugh. "At least a third of us have the cycle. No one's produced a Small yet." I pat her on the head. "I think you're going to be fine. But if you spontaneously make a Small, I'll assign it to someone else."

"Promise?"

"There have to be some advantages to being the Head Girl."

We walk in tandem, Quinn awkwardly mindful of the grassy wad planted between her legs, the inevitable snag and pull in her stomach. The air gets dense with salt the closer we get to the sea. When we finally reach the cliff's edge, the view is dizzying.

"Think we can scale it?" Quinn asks.

"Not without rope. I say we tuck into the wood a bit, build a shelter, and get a fire going."

"I was hoping we'd catch a fish."

"From up here?"

She shrugs.

We follow the edge until we reach a network of immature, ropey trees, a forest in progress, poking through the inhospitable rock with admirable determination.

Quinn tugs on a branch. "Let's just do a simple A-frame."

I agree. She passes me the ax and I take down the only tree tall enough to prop over the *A*. We work in exhausted silence, dragging our limbs, tying, fixing, layering. Though I work up a sweat, the air has cooled by a few degrees, as it does by the water.

"You got any pitch? I can't find the lighter."

"I do," Quinn says proudly. "Yanked this beauty off a tree when I went to pee."

"So your cycle *is* good for something." I take a darkened ball of sap from her and push on it with my fingers. "I'll work on a fire."

Quinn continues flinging branches over the A-frame until it resembles a tidy cocoon. It doesn't take long to get a fire going. The nesting material is dry and plentiful, the notch in the fireboard perfectly cut, the depth exact. I blow hard on the smoking nest and quickly transfer it to the heap of kindling Quinn's assembled. Its warmth is immediate.

"I'm dead," Quinn announces, lying facedown, arms by her side.

"I know." I reconfigure the firewood until the flames cooperate, shooting upward into a satisfying peak. Art. I lay beside Quinn. She drapes an arm over me and readjusts, so I feel her breath on my neck as if it's a light illuminating the *Colony* stamp embedded in my skin.

I close my eyes, willing the girls to be okay, acknowledging that I have no idea what's happening on the Hill but finding solace in having seen it from the cell tower, quiet and still-there, babies or not. It was not on fire. It didn't reek of sadness. It didn't shriek or call out. It was just there.

My back hurts from the tussle with Roman. My mind goes back to the cliffs, back to the moment our bodies made contact, the clashing of bones, the shifting of weight, the incredible hardness of the earth, unforgiving.

Quinn kisses the back of my neck, barely. A rebellious heat courses through my body.

I recall the violence, alive in my cuts. The warnings and threats. The warmth of fresh blood, the ache of crushed tissue. Blue's voice. Clover's. The bear tree in the woods. *They're coming*, Harlow missing, a wandering waif. Arrow back at camp, without me. The cutting fuzz of the radio, like teeth through water. The silence. The Colony.

The Mainland is low on girls.

And yet in the glow of the fire, the air rank with the ocean's secrets, it's him I think of. The width of his hands, the language of his eyes, his weight suffocating, his weight pleasing. Roman. Off the Hill in the middle of nowhere, I think of him. My body thinks of him.

CHAPTER 12

Section 2.1 - The Hill is a clandestine operation.

THE STIFFNESS IN my legs is like nothing I've ever experienced. Mornings after a particularly good haul of collecting have left me with a strained back or sore muscles, but today, my bone marrow aches. Quinn is still asleep. I force myself up, first to my knees and then to my feet, staggering like I'm on a boat. The fire is out and the perimeter rocks are cool. I'm starving. I lean down and tuck a piece of Quinn's hair behind her ear. My finger grazes her shoulder, bare and bruised.

I remember how the first time we met, she'd come out of the forest roaring, burlap pants cinched high on her waist, a dead snake clutched in her hand, smile on her face. So much has changed.

I slip into the sparse woods to look for anything edible, my fingers electric. I find fireweed. When I return, Quinn is up, stretching at the edge of the cliff, lit by the rising sun.

Beautiful.

"Morning," I say, waving a stalk of fireweed. "I got breakfast."

She points downward. "I need moss."

I nod toward where I came from. "Grass works too."

She raises her brows and passes me, yawning, legs pinched. I take apart the A-frame while I wait, surveying the area. It is quiet. No movement, spare a few birds and mosquitos. When she returns, we eat the fireweed in silence and clean the remainder of our site.

"We're going home," I say, sorting my pack.

"Without Harlow."

I stop. "We tried."

"Did we?"

"What's that supposed to mean?"

She shrugs. "We didn't make it very far."

"Yeah, and look at us. I'm surprised you can even see out of that eye, and I can barely walk."

"So it's true, what the Manual says—'*outside of the Hill's boundary, girls cannot survive.*'"

"We haven't *not* survived," I argue. "We're still alive." I stare at Quinn's swollen eye and gnarled cheek, at the filthy wrap on her hand. "Sort of."

"What are we going to tell them when we get back? The girls."

I'd been trying not to think about that because I don't know. Am I supposed to apologize? Lie? Tell them Harlow's dead, so they fall in line?

"And what about the boys?"

"No way. No one can know about them. If someone

looks at your face and asks what happened, you fell on the rocks. No one can know anything until we've figured this out."

Quinn cinches the cord on her bag, throws it over her shoulder, and picks up her spear. "You ready?"

I finish braiding my hair and haul a flat rock near the remnants of the fire. "My teeth feel disgusting."

Instinctively, Quinn runs her tongue across her top teeth.

I take a piece of charred wood, scrape the ends onto the rock, and break it down with my knife. "Grab me a stick."

Quinn finds a piece of unused kindling, snaps it in half, and peels off the bark. She chews the end and hands me the other. I do the same, biting until the end is frayed like washed-up sea rope. When the charcoal is fine enough, we dip the broken ends of our sticks into it and brush our teeth. We spit in opposite directions.

"Now are you ready?"

I rinse my mouth and spit again. Quinn hides the rock in the woods and then pitches both used sticks over the side of the cliff. "It's going to be hot," she says, eyeing the sun. "How long do you think this'll take?"

"I'm guessing we'll be there by late afternoon? Depends on the terrain. If it keeps up like this, maybe earlier."

For a while, we walk single-file, periodically leaning over to watch the ocean below, nipping and charging at the cliffs in a white fury. At times, I think I spot the slick head of a gray seal, the shadow of a whale that never breaches, the outline of a boat, the 105th floor of a lost skyscraper. Structures we've read about but exist only in our imagination. I never know the truth.

By the time the sun is directly overhead, the landscape begins to change. "I feel like we're going down." I pause to look over the side of the cliff. "See?" I point. "We could probably scale this."

Quinn steadies herself on the edge and holds onto my arm as she leans forward to assess the drop. "If my hand was normal, we could." She removes the makeshift bandage and tries to make a fist, but her fingers resist.

"Then we'll go a little further. If we keep descending, it should get easier."

"I'm hungry."

"I know. I still have fiddleheads in my bag, and there should be some more lingonberries around here."

"I need protein."

"We can fish when we get down there. We can't from here."

Quinn stops, tipping the water container upside down. A drop hits her front tooth.

"We're out of water."

"What do you mean, we're out of water? Seriously?" I sigh. "There was a stream back at the clearing."

"That's way too far," she says, slouching against a sapling that can barely hold her weight. She pushes away, righting herself, and looks up at the sky. "Doesn't look like any chance of showers."

I nod toward the forest. "Our best bet is to go down."

"Or we could dig a well?"

"Not here we can't." I grind my foot into the ground. "It's solid rock. We have to go back to the woods. Follow the birds."

"That never works for me."

"Because you slingshot them. The whole island's bird population probably knows it. They flee when they see you coming."

"*You* don't mind eating them."

"They taste better than crickets." I put my hand to my ear, but only hear the ocean. Not helpful. "If you can't follow the birds, then chase the insects."

"Ugh," she grunts. "You see how many bites I have?"

"They'll lead you to a water source."

"That's not all they'll do." She shows off a string of welts on her forearm.

I try to swallow, my mouth dry as a summer forest. "You must have known we were almost out of water."

Quinn stops. "Me?" she gestures. "Why would it be my responsibility?"

"You have the canteen."

"You were the last one to drink from it."

I throw up my hands. "What are you talking about? You just took the last sip." I attempt to lick my lips.

"That was one drop. You drank from it by the cell tower."

I have no idea if what she's saying is accurate. How do I not remember? How do I have zero recollection? All I know is thirst. My vision bends. "You had it last," I mutter.

Quinn hurls the canteen at a tree. It misses and bounces off a rock, causing a pleasing clink that reverberates through the edge of the wood.

"That was mature."

"And whining like a Small is any different?" She points a scabbed finger. "The food might have been on me, but the water's on both of us. What does the Manual say about water? Section 2.7. '*Water is* . . .'"

"Shut up about the Manual." It comes out more aggressively than I expect. I cover my ears with my hands, fingernails digging into my scalp.

Quinn takes a step back. "Wren, calm down."

Tears stream down my face, and I collapse into a childish heap. Quinn takes a measured step forward and reaches for the top of my head, like she might pet me. I bat her hand away.

"We'll find water," she says, eyes darting, as if she wishes there was a witness. "The Colony—"

"Don't talk about the Colony."

Quinn spits. "Is there anything I *can* say?"

"Tell me I'm not crazy."

She makes a face, the kind Smalls make when they're weighing between two possible answers, stressing over which one they think is more desirable. "Crazy for . . ."

"For not knowing anything right now."

"Well, you know—"

"Nothing. We know nothing. The Colony lied to us. Look at these rocks, Quinn? They're just normal rocks." I pound the surface with the heel of my hand. "What is going *on*?"

"Maybe the rocks were dangerous at one time."

"Or not. Maybe they were always just rocks." A tear drops from my cheek, staining the ground black.

"If the Colony didn't want us here, it's for own protection."

"Protection from what?"

"Boys, bears . . . disease? I don't know."

"Exactly. You don't know." I grab her wrist and pull myself to my feet, avoiding a beetle with a shiny back. "We don't know anything."

"False. We don't know *every*thing. Sometimes the truth can't be digested all at once. You wouldn't eat a deer in one sitting; it would be too much. You'd get sick. You wouldn't be able to keep it down. You wouldn't be able to process it. It's the same reason the Manual's in sections. You move through it, piece by piece, one truth at a time."

One truth, or one lie? "Until?"

"The Departure Ceremony. Until we get to the Colony."

"And what if we don't make it there?"

Quinn searches her sleeve for a hint of unscathed fabric and swipes her forearm across my cheeks. "You're not crazy."

WE PROCEED IN silence, Quinn at the front, clawing our way through the brush until we find a game trail, a good indication that it may eventually lead to fresh water—hopefully flowing. I concentrate on things that are real to recalibrate my brain. Things that are known. Things that are true. *Ambystoma gracile*, Northwestern salamander—real. I see one on the rock in front of me, eyes unblinking, body the color of a rusted can. It bolts and disappears in a jumble of brush. Dandelion—real. I swipe my hand across the dense velvet petals, causing the weed's stem to sway. I examine the faint yellow blot left behind on my fingertip, then look up at the sky and circle my arms, the air thick as soup—dragonfly, real; toadstool—real; Quinn—real. I snap off a tree branch, the end jagged, and stab it into my hand with feral violence. The impact takes me out at the knees. I gasp, a silent scream, as a tidal pool of blood forms in my palm. Real. I drop the stick before Quinn even turns around. Onward.

We meander through a depression and pass over a dead tree. "What do you make of Roman's comment?" I blurt. "That the Mainland's low on girls?"

"Dunno, Wren. Maybe there's a disease there that only affects girls and is killing them off."

"Like what?"

"Lyme disease?"

"I think anyone can get that."

"Maybe they all bled to death from the cycle."

"It's not that bad."

"You said the same thing about grubs."

"That was once. But if you really want protein, I can find some for you."

"No thanks. I'd eat skunk cabbage before I ever eat another grub."

"Suit yourself," I say, trekking deeper into the wood, the trees ancient and sprawling.

In a snap second, Quinn drops her spear and pulls an arrow from the quiver strapped to her back. She steadies her bow, wincing in pain. I face the direction she's pointing in, trying to see what she sees, but it's a blur of leaves, heavy and green.

"Damn it," she says, before she even has a chance to draw back her elbow.

"What was it?"

"A rabbit."

I place a hand on her back. "Maybe it went for water," I offer. "Hear that?"

She listens and nods. We scramble upward and pass over a crest before loping back down. A stream weaves through the landscape at a hurried pace, tumbling over rocks, splashing at will.

"We should filter it," Quinn says, squatting on the tiny bank and handing me the container.

"No time." I tip the mouth of the canteen into the water, letting it run over my knuckles.

Quinn washes her face. "We should try the girls again. Let them know we're on our way back."

"Hand me the radio."

She rummages through her pack, her eye nearly swollen shut, rugged as a scavenger, beautiful as the summer solstice. She fumbles, nearly dropping the device in the water. My heart sinks and recovers.

"Wren to Clover," I say, careful to articulate each syllable. "Are you there? Over."

We listen keenly for a response, turning our backs to the stream, willing it to shut up. A long, drawn-out *shhh* sound penetrates the forest and pierces our ears. Feedback.

Quinn winces, covering her head. "Turn it down."

I lower the volume to three. The feedback stops abruptly.

"We're too far," Quinn rationalizes. "That thing's a piece of junk. Doesn't even work from the Hunter's Cabin to the Rock. And the batteries haven't been replaced in months, maybe a year. When's the last time the Colony sent batteries?"

"It's been a while. The Arrival before the most recent one."

"The one even before that," she argues, spitting aimlessly to the side. "What's going on over there?"

The radio kicks to life, the *shhh* sound resuming, this time at a higher pitch. We both try to bat it away. "Shut it off." Quinn rips a fern out of the ground. "Let's go."

"Where are you going?" A whisper.

I drop the radio and cower like it might cut me. Quinn's eyes bulge, her breath shortening. She steps on the radio, trying to silence the voice. I dive beneath her foot and switch it off.

"What was that, Wren? Who said that?"

I shake my head. "Check the frequency."

"It's on *A*," she says, turning it in her hand. "As it should be."

"Probably a drifter from the Mainland."

"Not a chance."

"The village?"

She gathers the stuff strewn around the bank of the stream. "The Hill," she says quietly. "We both know it came from the Hill."

CHAPTER 13

Section 2.1 – Nobody knows about the Hill or the Colony.

WE STAMP ANXIOUSLY through the forest back toward the shore, urgency quickening our steps until the trees thicken and we're forced to snake through, the pace dismal. I stop short, the cliff a good twenty feet away, and grab a branch. It barely moves. "Should we climb?" I ask, testing another.

Quinn gazes toward the cliff and then faces north. "It'd be nice if we could get a visual." She kneels. "Step on my back."

I place my foot in the meaty space between her shoulder blades and spine. She doesn't flinch; doesn't even make a sound when I transfer my entire weight onto her back, heavier than yesterday. "Thanks," I grunt, pulling myself up onto the second branch. When I cut through the canopy, I look down and am alarmed by how high I've climbed.

"Do you see anything?" Quinn hollers.

"I don't know yet." I shift so my back is against the trunk and inch forward, using an overhead limb as a guide. The view is dizzying.

"Well?"

"I can see the ocean."

"So can I," Quinn says, eating something she's picked. She leans against the tree.

I part a clump of leaves and see the beach. Our beach. I recognize the adjacent cliffs, the cave where we store our fishing gear, and the distinct arc of sand, a perfect waxing crescent. Empty boats are tethered offshore. "I see the beach."

I start to retreat when something knocks me off-balance. I grab the limb above me, my arm flexed at a rigid ninety-degree angle. My legs weaken. I cover my mouth with my free hand.

A boy comes out of the cave.

Why is there a boy on our beach?

He is far bigger than Roman. His stomach resembles a turtle shell that bulges below his chest. His hair is black and streaked gray on his chin, kinked and disheveled.

Quinn whistles. "Anything?" Her tone reflects a growing impatience.

The boy looks up in our direction. He's old. He's lived.

"Shh," I whisper into the air, recoiling into a squat. "He can hear us."

Quinn walks around the tree, her eyes fixed upward in an effort to locate me. Before she has a chance to say anything, I motion my finger to my lips. She looks alarmed and pulls her spear.

I gesture for her to climb up, but she mouths *I can't,* nodding to the gear slung over each shoulder and raising her busted fist.

"You have to try," I mouth, tears breaching. "He can *hear us.*"

"Who's he?" She cups her hands around her mouth as though she might prevent her words from falling on foreign ears. Her eyes dart.

"I don't know who he is. Just hand me the stuff."

She leans her spear against the tree, wrestles the packs off her back, and passes them to me in succession. In the distance, I hear the forest floor come alive with movement. *Hurry up,* I mouth.

She tosses the spear next. I stick it into the branch and then tighten my grip on the tree, squeezing my thighs, my ankles crossed and dangling like a bony knot. "You have to climb." I'm barely audible. "Reach."

I wrap my hands around her forearm and pull. She throws her bad arm around a branch for support, feet swiping against the trunk. Together, we muscle her up. The veins running through my arms inflate blue. When she's in the tree, we scramble with our gear to get a higher position, adrenaline driving us upward. Squirrels seeking higher ground.

About two-thirds of the way up, the footsteps become louder. Instead of hearing intermittent snaps, we hear a pattern. Consistent, deliberate steps. I hold my breath, my chest pressed up against the tree, and inch toward the side facing the beach. It takes several painstaking minutes before I get a visual—bushy hair not unlike Quinn's, a large stomach, a sophisticated pack strapped on his back. A water bottle dangles from a cord. It makes me aware of my thirst, my throat a desert. I didn't drink enough. Why hadn't I taken more?

He paces through the trees, periodically glancing at a handheld instrument. He moves haphazardly, like he's never been in the woods before, zigzagging left and right, circling, never looking up. This can't be someone from Roman's village. At one point, he passes beneath the far-reaching tips of the tree we're hiding in and heads toward the cliff, still looking down at the device in his hand. I glance at Quinn, one branch below. She covers her mouth with both hands, a trick her Mother probably taught her to keep quiet, always on guard. Just in case.

When he reaches the edge of the cliff, I exhale messily, aware of how much of my breath I'd been holding hostage. Quinn breathes too, her hands still up in her face so she can shut her mouth in an instant. The stranger holds the device near his ear as if listening to something, and it occurs to me it's some type of communication device.

I instinctively reach into my pocket, feeling for the radio. Do I have it or does Quinn? I do. Is it turned on? I fiddle with the gears, spin the dial. I can't tell if I've just switched it off or turned up the volume. I wait, counting in my head. Nothing.

I exhale, relieved, and then shrill shrieking spills from my pocket. I panic, pull out the cursed radio, the feedback blaring, and frantically shut it off. I look toward the stranger on the cliff's edge.

He buries his own device between his hands and looks in our direction, waiting for the next screech of feedback to disturb the silence, but the rock beneath his feet gives way. In one horrific second, he falls backward over the cliff.

CHAPTER 14

Section 6.2 - For head injuries and other trauma, do not attempt to move the body.

ON THE GROUND, moving feels different. My legs wobble with adrenaline, and a wave of sickness passes over me, inebriating my steps like the force of a magnet on the needle of a compass. Quinn stumbles into me as we make our way to the edge of the cliff. She gags before we get there, collapsing her hands on her knees. A thread of saliva blows from her chin like spider silk, detaching and landing on her leg.

Ditching my pack, I get on my stomach and drag myself toward the fragmented lip, unsure whether more of the cliff will give way. Debris collects underneath my neck and digs into my collarbone. I wrap my fingertips around the edge of the cliff on rock that seems ancient and unlikely to move and pull myself far enough forward that my forehead and eyes peer over the top. I look down at him, the boy who doesn't look boyish, his legs twisted, arms too.

Blood pools in a crevice to the left of his head. My mind records the image: the awkward position of his bent right leg, the spread of hair extending from his head like the flames of a well-fed fire. He lies in the back of my brain, and then I see movement. It is slight. His cheek, which is pressed to the side, lifts, and he slowly turns his head. It is so slow. I actually count: one-one thousand, two-one thousand. We make eye contact at four.

"He's alive," I say to Quinn, who crawls over, wiping the sweat off her face with her bare arm, her cheeks flushed.

"You sure?"

"We made eye contact."

She stretches out beside me, fumbling toward the edge of the cliff. We look down. She makes a sound akin to a wheeze and pulls back. Like me, she's seen his trembling hand, outstretched, barely afloat, searching for help.

"We need to get down there." I hit the cliff with the heel of my hand. It feels solid. "We can scale this."

"But what if it collapses? We shouldn't risk our lives to kill him if he's going to die anyway."

"Kill him? We need to *help* him."

"What the hell is wrong with you?" Her eyes blaze. "Section 8.3. *'If you encounter a boy, take swift and violent action to eliminate him.'*"

"This is different, Quinn. He's suffering." I pause. "Need I remind you about the time you didn't use a heavy enough rock for your deadfall trap? It took weeks to get the sound of that coyote's cry out of my head."

"Don't talk about that." She points to her eye. "He's not the only one suffering. We should have killed the boys in the woods, and we should kill him too."

"Roman didn't do anything to hurt us."

"Is that what you call him now? By his first name? He might not have done anything to you, but my face thinks differently." She points to the gap from her knocked-out tooth.

"That was Finn. Besides, you struck first."

"Because I followed the rules!"

"You didn't follow them the first time when you were out chasing deer with Odessa."

"WE WERE STARVING!" she spits. "What are you *doing*, Wren? He was on our beach. In sixty-seven years, no one has come to the Hill. And we both know that wasn't a girl on the other end of the radio back there." She shakes her head, turns in a circle, and mutters, "I knew this would happen."

My jaw clenches. "You knew *what* would happen?"

"That you'd fail. That somehow you'd mess this whole thing up. Sixty-seven years." She looks over the cliff. "You can't keep making naive decisions. Save Harlow! Save the boy!"

"You're saying that doing what's right makes me a failure?"

"Is that what you're doing, Wren? What's right? Do you really think that?"

"No, Quinn. I don't think it; I *feel* that it's the right

128

thing to do, but since you asked, I'll tell you what I *think*, and that is if it was you who took over for Beck, we'd all have probably gone over a cliff by now. ON PURPOSE."

"At least Harlow wouldn't have been dragged off alone. That only happens when *you're* in charge."

A shockwave of emotion rips through me. "I . . . I can't believe you would say that."

"It's no worse than what you said to me." A tear rolls down her cheek. "Th-that girls would kill themselves if I'd been left in charge?"

"I didn't mean it that way."

"In what other way could you possibly have meant it? I know I'm not the most likeable girl. I know I have a temper and that I don't always think before I speak and that I don't look like Nova or have a quirky patch or patience or a beautiful singing voice, but I love you!"

She snatches her pack, swings it over her shoulder, and turns away.

I head in the opposite direction, numb, sorry, and confused. Love?

I look over the edge at the mass of human below, barely alive. How can she talk about love right now? He looks harmless. But a part of me worries she's right. A boy on the beach—insanity. I think of Beck's map, the red arrows thicker than fists, pointing to the Hill. The sightings. The voice on the radio, faint, deep. I storm off.

"Where are you going?" Quinn rushes after me. "I thought we were going down?"

"We are going down. It took him no time to get up here. There has to be an easier way than scaling. A path."

"Then how come we've never seen it before?"

"Because until I made one of my 'naive decisions,' we weren't *allowed* here!"

Quinn flinches but says nothing. Minutes into our descent, we reach a spot with a visible ledge about six feet down. "We can jump to there"—I point—"and then again to the bottom."

I drop my pack, swing my legs over the side, and lower myself down, my pelvis crashing into the rock face. I curse before letting go and landing on the shelf. "Pass me my pack."

Quinn slides our gear down to me, followed by her spear, and then lands beside me with matched clumsiness. We face the water frothing below. It's a big jump. My stomach seizes, and then Quinn leaps off erratically, but lands safely with an audible thud. I toss everything down and follow suit.

Quinn charges forward, rounding a slight bend in the rock.

But I love you. Her words ping inside my head. Should I have known? Before I can even process the question, she returns, looking like she's seen her own death.

"What?"

"He's—he's gone."

"What do you mean, *gone*?" I scramble to my feet, my legs breaking into a run before my body is even erect. I round the corner, assuming Quinn's got it wrong, that she miscalculated the location of his fall.

But she hasn't. There's nothing on the rock but a handful of mussels and a pool of blood.

SOMETHING'S NOT RIGHT. "Where could he have gone?" I spin in a circle, looking for clues.

Quinn stares at the crashing waves. "I don't think he would have gone in the water," she says. "Unless he wanted to drown himself."

"But if he just wanted to die, he wouldn't have reached up for help."

Quinn shrugs. "No way he could have walked. Both of his legs looked broken."

"Someone had to have moved him."

"Wren, look around. There's nowhere to even go."

It's true. There's water and a cliff. Neither option makes sense. I survey the ground for more blood. "Here." I find a spot the size of a cloverleaf.

"That could just be spatter from when he fell."

I tuck the loose hairs from my braid behind my ears and press forward, eyes to the shore, away from the area we scaled down. The space narrows, but I find another drop of blood. I don't say anything to Quinn, afraid to take my eyes off the ground.

I arrive at a point where the rock floor narrows, and the cliff juts out like an arrowhead. I gesture for Quinn to join me.

Avoiding the waves, we pass around the arrowhead to the other side, where the ground opens up again.

"What is that?" Quinn points to a crack in the side of the cliff. It's not significant—nothing like the cave on our beach, which is at least ten girls wide and set far enough away from the water that it does its job storing gear and keeping it dry. I stop at the opening. It's just wide enough for me to stand with my arms straight out from my shoulders, my palms able to press firmly on either side.

"Your arms are really long," Quinn says behind me.

I spin around. "They are not. No longer than anyone else's."

She shrugs, and for a second I'm distracted. Are they the same length as everyone else's, or are they in fact *really* long? Freakishly long, like a pair of oars? And even if they are freakishly long, so what? It just means I can reach more, hit harder. Or I'm deformed.

"Look," Quinn says. She pulls a piece of hair off the side of the rock, from where my palm had been pressed. Another tendril of evidence.

"It's a tunnel." I clench my fists together, overcome with the discovery. "We need torches."

"Did you find the lighter? We used all the pitch."

I search my pack and find it wedged inside a pocket, a rectangular piece of plastic, orange and scuffed. Quinn navigates the shoreline, stopping at a dead tree that sticks out from between the rocks like it's been squeezed to death. I test the lighter. Collectors often find them on the Hill, but they need fluid to work, and most are cracked or empty. I roll my thumb over the metal wheel. It leaves tiny troughs and traces of rust on my skin.

Quinn passes me one of the branches. She's gathered bits of bark and fragments of debris from around the tree. Without animal fat, they won't stay lit for long.

"Here." I pull the shirt we'd found in the Collector's bag out of my pack. I tear it into thick strips, and Quinn fills the pieces of fabric with the bark and then ties them on the end of each stick. When she's finished, she hands me the straight one and keeps the inferior one for herself. I trade back. "You lead. I need to think."

I light her torch first and then mine. Both take a second to stay lit, and then Quinn steps into the darkness. Her chest is proud, but her feet remain cautious as she walks with the same foot always in the lead, the second foot always playing catch-up. Step, pause, step, pause. There's nothing on the walls or the ceilings above. Only a bit of loose rock scuffs beneath our feet. It is cold and the air old, as though from another time, like it was trapped inside a trunk, stagnant and slightly damp. Goosebumps ripple across my arms.

I don't realize I'm lagging behind until Quinn grabs my hand. We link our fingers into a tight ball and proceed further into the tunnel. It turns a sharp right and to my relief, widens, so we can walk comfortably, shoulder-to-shoulder. I've lost all sense of distance and space. I can't tell whether we have taken eight paces or eighty. I should have been counting.

"Hello?" someone hollers from behind. Quinn and I freeze. Another boy. "Anybody in here?"

How can there be another? Where are they coming from?

She mock-blows on her torch. I nod, and together we extinguish our flames, then, still holding hands, we slide down on the left wall and cower, the voice getting closer.

CHAPTER 15

Section 5.5 – Girls must protect the Hill
or die trying. The Colony applauds your
sacrifice.

WE WAIT IN the blackness for a long time, well after
the voice fades, never getting close enough for us to
see who it belonged to. I fiddle with the lighter in my
pocket, cursing the defective wheel as I try a dozen
times to get it lit. When I do, the flame is miniature and
mostly blue. "Come on." When we both have light, we
trek deeper into the tunnel. What if we get blocked in?

"Now what?" Quinn asks as we reach a fork in the
path. "Left or right?"

I head left and examine the entrance for a clue.
There are no visible markings. No directional arrows or
instructions. Where is a manual when you need one? I
squeeze my eyes shut and strive for an intuitive sense,
but I get nothing. I go to the right and do the same thing,
checking first with my physical senses, and second with
my instincts. "This way." I point right.

Quinn nods and joins me. She doesn't ask for an explanation, and I don't tell her that I made the decision purely because there's an R in my name and no L. Maybe she's right about my naive decision-making, but only twelve steps in—twelve because I remembered to count this time—we find him.

We see the soles of his tan boots first. Large and bulbous, they flop to either side, pulling his knees with them. His stomach looks less distended from this viewpoint, and I notice he's wearing a vest.

"Looks like he was carried," Quinn says, her eyes fixed on his arms, which are indeed over his head, like he'd been dragged. I think of Arrow's last recollection of Harlow being removed from the Hill. I swallow, forcing the emotions down, and kneel beside the motionless person who looks more like a washed-up sea creature than a human. His right leg is undoubtedly broken, the bone jutting out like a gnarled root. I scan his body, looking for the rise and fall of his chest, but I can't tell if it's moving. I lean in toward his face, peeling back a section of blood-soaked hair to uncover his ear, which is large and eel-like in the dim light.

I whisper, "Are you alive? Are you okay? Can you hear me?" His paper-thin lids flutter, opening just wide enough to reveal the milky white of his eyes.

Section 6.1. COMPRESSIONS. I locate the center of his chest, place my hands on top of each other, lock my arms, and start pushing up and down. Clover saved a Small this way. The force was nearly unbearable to watch, but the girl survived, eventually sputtering out a third of the ocean and a lifetime of bile. But something feels wrong. His chest is not hard. There is an ominous softness to his body. His rib cage feels like a patchwork of broken shells and wet sand. I feel myself start to cry, a sneezy tingle.

Quinn jumps in and takes over. But after what seems to be a hundred repetitions, she shakes her head. The rhythm of her compressions changes from fast and frenetic to slow and deliberate. A death march. And then they stop.

"He's dead," she says matter-of-factly, leaning back on her heels, unable to mask a look of relief. She wipes sweat from her face, but I wipe tears. My faulty C-shaped torch slips from where it balances against the wall, and I jump to reset it before it lights my pack on fire.

"We tried." Quinn shrugs.

I continue to cry, sniffing.

She stares at me, annoyed. "Wren, he's the enemy. Why else would he have been on our beach?"

"That's just it, Quinn. We don't know why he was there."

"But it doesn't matter. He's a boy—that's enough."

He's only the fourth boy I've seen outside of the Manual sketches. He looks nothing like Roman or the other two. He's not from around here. Definitely older, face creased and weathered, hands worn, his skin the same color as Beck, as Quinn.

I readjust my patch, aware of the effort it takes just to lift my arms, which feel like jellyfish after the effort to revive him. But then Quinn and I hear a faint groan.

I know she hears it too, because we lock eyes. And it's coming from *him*, deep within. As if what's left of him, the infinitesimal amount of life left, calls out. A shadow of his younger self. A boy, buried deep beneath layers of fat and flesh and life.

He cries out, his arm reaching up a few desperate inches, a final plea to live.

Once again, I place my hands on his chest and press down into the wet sand, his ribs like buried sticks. But ten compressions in, I'm violently hauled off.

A forearm wraps around my neck while a hand covers my gaping mouth, pressing against my nostrils so I can barely breathe. I reach my hands up to remove the arm, but my attempt is futile, and instead, I collapse my chin into my chest, protecting the tiny space left that allows me to breathe. Out of the corner of my eye, I note that Quinn's met a similar fate, but unlike me, she puts up a violent fight.

My heart thumps inside my rib cage. With a surge of adrenaline, I peel away the hand covering my mouth one finger at a time. Then I twist my head inward toward my assailant and pry her arm away. She gives in, her arms slumping by her sides.

Blue, looking gray in the torchlight, stares back at me, exhausted.

"What the hell?" I shout, recovering my breath.

"You were trying to save him." She nudges his body with her foot. "The enemy."

Across from us, Quinn has also been released. Lennon stands proudly beside her, face cut and covered in dirt. Quinn, visibly agitated, adjusts her kinked shirt and jumps to her feet with animal-like agility.

"It's wrong to let someone die when the possibility of saving him exists," I say.

"I'll tell you what's wrong." Blue places her finger on my breastbone with such force it pushes me back into the wall. "What's wrong is *you* running off to find Harlow and leaving the rest of *us* to fight off an ambush." She pauses to wipe spit from her face. "An ambush that included that boy-man-*thing* you were trying to bring back to life."

An ambush?

The warnings were true. The map and the sightings and the rumors. I should have listened. Assigned more to defense.

I should never have left.

"I couldn't have predicted an attack," I argue, pushing my shoulders off the wall. "And I came back."

"You came back," Blue repeats. "The savior of the Hill has returned." She reminds me of Quinn, all rage and temper. Goes for the juglar. A Hunter.

Quinn steps over the body and places her hands on Blue's shoulders. She whispers something that neither Lennon nor I can make out, but whatever she says is effective. Blue exhales a diffusing breath.

"Lennon, stay with him. I don't know how much time he has left, but whatever the amount, it'll be dignified. Blue, tell me everything that's happened since we left. Where is everyone? Where are the Smalls? Is everyone accounted for?" My questions come out like bullets, the growing horror of the situation crippling. The very notion that we're talking over a body who half of us want dead sickens me.

"Where's Arrow?" It comes out as a scream, and all three girls look at me, wide-eyed.

"Arrow's fine," Lennon says. "Most of the Smalls were napping when the Arrival Signal appeared, Arrow included. Clover let them stay behind with the Mothers while the rest of us went down to the beach to get the babies."

I cut her off. "But the boats were empty."

"Y-yes," Blue stutters. "Clover and a few other girls waded into the water to get the boats, but when they reached them, they were bare. No babies. No supplies, either. That's what we were trying to tell you over the radio."

"Where's the radio now?"

"No idea. Lost it."

Quinn and I exchange glances.

"Then all of a sudden, we were surrounded by these people," Lennon says, face animated, hands flying for effect. "They came out of the woods, out of the cave. They were on top of the cliff."

"People started running," Blue adds.

"A few of them were girls."

"Attacker girls?"

"Yes, girls!"

Where in the Manual does it say anything about enemy girls?

I shake my head in disbelief. "Did they . . . say anything?"

"He did." Blue gestures to the man on the ground. "He said the Colony left them no choice."

"No choice for what?" Quinn wipes blood from her mouth.

Lennon shrugs.

"Well, that's helpful." I sigh. "Where is everyone right now?"

"The Mothers and the Smalls escaped into the Westside Forest. They're in the old Hunter's Cabin, I think."

The Hunter's Cabin near the boundary is about a hundred years old and in ruin. You can't see the roof for sky, and the floor is alive with insects.

"So far, we think they're safe."

I feel a temporary high of relief. Arrow is safe.

Blue continues, "They lined everyone up else on the beach, asked if anyone was missing, and then sent them uphill and told them to pack their stuff."

"For what?"

"I don't know. They didn't say."

Quinn crosses her arms. "You don't order someone to pack up their stuff if you don't plan on taking them somewhere."

"But how did you escape?"

"We swam," Blue says.

"And no one noticed? I find that hard to believe."

Lennon whispers, "No one saw Harlow."

Quinn raises her eyebrows.

"We just went for it," Lennon explains. "There was a moment when they were sort of conferring and trying to figure of what to do, and they were all crowded

141

around the cave. We both dove in and as soon as we got far enough . . ."

"We swam out past the cliff and climbed ashore." Blue shows off a fresh wound on her shin. "It's fricking rocky out there."

"'Fricking?'"

She points. "That's what he said."

I look down at the body. Fricking rocky. No kidding.

"We probably wouldn't have made it if we hadn't found the crack in this cliff." Lennon pats the wall affectionately. Gratitude.

"Anyone know you're here?"

"Not that we know of," Lennon replies.

Quinn exhales. "We heard a boy's voice minutes ago, on our way in."

"That's a first," Blue says. "We haven't seen anyone come this way—until him."

We all glare down at the body stretched between us. I imagine I hear a groan. I take what's left of the shirt we tore up to make the torches, fold it a few times, and place it under his head. "We need a plan."

"Shouldn't we do it away from him?" Blue asks.

Quinn nudges him with her foot. "I don't think he's going anywhere."

"No, she's right," I agree. "Where does this tunnel go?"

"Dead-end."

"What about the other one?"

"We don't know."

"But it's not a dead-end?"

"Not that we know of. It gets really narrow, and the only torch we had at the time was close to burning out."

"Lennon, stay with him. We'll be back."

"Alone?"

I hand her my knife and head in the direction of the fork, with Quinn and Blue jostling behind me. "How many are there? Besides him."

"We counted nine, but there could have been more on the Hill."

"If you've been here the whole time, how did you know about the Smalls and the Mothers in the woods?"

"We snuck out at night to get food. Clover was on the beach. She'd been sent down to check the gillnets."

"What, we're *feeding* them too?" Quinn scowls.

"What did she say?"

"Just that the Mothers were safe in the woods."

"Nothing else? Did she mention any plan?"

"We only had a minute before someone came down looking for her—a gaunt girl with half of her teeth missing and hair in patches."

"A girl? Seriously?" Boys. It's supposed to be boys. My mind races. I think of all the things the Manual said we couldn't surive: the Eastside Forest, Limestone Pass, boys. Girls? Maybe it's time *we* write the Manual. A feeling washes over me but doesn't leave, like salt after an ocean swim, filling my chest and restoring energy to my limbs, my extremities. It is power. Power and purpose.

"Let's get some sleep," I say. "Tomorrow, we take back our Hill."

CHAPTER 16

Section 3.7 – A helicopter is a type of air-craft that can be identified by rotor blades and a landing skid. They are sometimes visible in the sky. Ignore and avoid them.

THE NEXT MORNING, I awake to the sound of the stranger's device chirping inside his pocket. It repeats two or three times before going silent again. He makes no attempt to retrieve it. The other girls, a tangle of legs and ripped clothing, don't even flinch.

"Hey," I whisper in the darkness. There's no response. I find the lighter in my pocket, depress the rusted wheel, and get a tiny blue flame. "Thing's going to die," I say to myself as I locate my torch and light it.

"Wa-ter," he says, his voice so hoarse and faint I have to convince myself I've heard correctly.

I'm also parched. "I don't have any."

He attempts to speak again. His lips form an *O* the size of an acorn, but there is no sound.

The air is dank and smells like rot, the way an animal smells when the cause of death is unknown. The rest of the tunnel is earthy and damp. I lean my torch against the wall behind me to stand up and stretch. In my shadow, my arms do look ridiculously long.

I'll use the time to devise a plan. Figure out a way to take back the Hill. Make everything go back to the way it was.

I reach the fork, but instead of heading out of the tunnel back toward the crack in the cliff, where there's light and air and a chance of food, I make a sharp turn and step into the beckoning mouth of the left tunnel. It is only slightly less wide than the other, but after a minute, it winds to the left and narrows as Blue described. I hyperventilate as it closes in on my shoulders, leaving only inches on either side. Though nothing touches me, I feel the weight of my surroundings. A rock blanket. In a few steps, I am forced to continue shoulder-first, my chest and back now facing either side of the path, my torch and patched eye leading the way. Why didn't I bring Quinn? I say to myself. This is ridiculous. I can barely move. There's nothing here.

Despite my internal dialogue, my feet continue to tread deeper into the labyrinth. Ahead, the tunnel shrinks down to a mere hole. I decide that if I'm forced to continue on my stomach and slither through like a snake, I'm turning back.

But it's not like that. As the ceiling dips, my spine drags across the roof, drawing blood. I don't know if I'm mistaking the warm, wet sensation of blood with the glow of light, but as I move forward, it seems to be getting brighter. Either that, or my eye has evolved at micro-speed to operate underground, like a mole's.

The next section widens, with parts steep enough that I half-crawl, half-scramble until the ground flattens again. I have déjà vu, as if I've traveled it before. Impossible—and yet a recollection flashes in the back of my brain: Small me, barefoot, no bigger than Arrow, hustling through a tunnel. The Colony?

Eventually, the whole path opens up gradually, in great sloping curves. I slip on loose rocks and drop my torch, but I manage to stay upright, surfing down the side into space. I tighten my stomach to try to maintain control of my flailing body, but I begin to fall. I reach forward, waiting for the impact, expecting my rib cage to bounce off the rock, but midway down, a figure appears and breaks my fall.

My legs skid to a stop in opposite directions. My arms remain wrapped around the trunk of the stranger who intercepted my fate. I hold on for dear life, trying to catch my breath and steady my feet simultaneously.

Then, as quick as the fall itself, I'm standing on my own, face-to-face with Roman. My heart flickers, spontaneous and loud. I place my hand on my chest as if to keep it from exploding. What is happening?

"You okay?" he asks.

"Yes," I reply, both pleased and disturbed. I use the opportunity to check out my surroundings. A cave. Light leaks in from a network of cracks above us. I climb back up the incline from where I crashed down and retrieve what's left of my dying torch, opting this time to slide down on my butt. Roman lights my path.

"It's a flashlight," he explains.

"I know. We've had them on the Hill before. The Colony's not very good at remembering to send batteries, though. Where'd you get it?"

He offers it out for me to hold. "Traded it once with someone from the Mainland."

I point the light around the cave, fascinated by the exactness of the beam, then I pass it back. He stares into my eye deeply, the way he did in the clearing before things got messy. It feels like a test, so I hold steady and stare back. His eyes, that mottled brown and green . . . I want to trust them.

"What are you doing here?" I ask. "How did you find this place?"

"These tunnels have been here for ages," he replies. "The Colony doesn't like us being here seeing that it's so close to the Hill, but that's what I find so fascinating. It's literally right next door, and not one of you knows it exists. No one so much as even stumbled upon the entrance of this tunnel—or any of the others."

There are others? I flash back to Quinn dangling over the black hole by the bear tree. Was that one?

"That's dedication," he adds.

"We follow the rules." Or used to.

He smiles. I sigh. Why is he smiling? Because we are a joke? Girls living on a dump, unaware of anything beyond our boundary and the Manual? Villages, tunnels, boys, the Mainland—and me, their Head Girl, on the job for less than three days, falling face-first out of a tunnel with no plan, no water, no clue. I want to hit him. Right in the mouth. Right in his beautiful smile.

Did I just think *beautiful* smile? What is happening?

"You have a beautiful smile," he says.

"Excuse me?"

"I said, what happened to your eye?"

I put my hand up over my patched eye. "This one?"

"Yes." He laughs. "That one."

I don't know what's wrong with me. "It's blind."

"Oh. Sorry."

I shake myself, as though the movement will somehow bring me out of my stupor. "What are you doing here?" I repeat. "How did you know we were here?"

"I came to find you," he says. "Conveniently, you left a trail of blood."

"What for?"

"The girl you said was missing."

"Harlow?"

"Brownish hair, kind of thin?"

"You've seen her?"

"No, but some of the boys did. There's an old helipad just south of us."

"What's a helipad?"

"A place where helicopters land and take off."

I stare at him, already disbelieving what it is coming next.

"She went to the Mainland."

"How? With who?" I exhale, trying to stop the panic. Maybe it was just the Colony. Maybe there was something wrong with Harlow and she needed to be removed.

"Can't answer that. Finn was checking a trap. Next thing you know, he hears a helicopter overhead. Unexpected."

I cut him off. "What do you mean, unexpected?"

"It wasn't on the schedule. Mainlanders fly in a few times a year for trade. Unless called for during a medical emergency, we're not supposed to see them for another few months."

"Then what?"

"According to him, the helicopter lands, and just as he's about to find out why, your girl steps out of the woods."

"With who?" I ask again, frantic.

"Some guy."

"That's it? Some guy?"

"That's all I got." He pauses. "Though Finn did say something interesting. There was a woman on the helicopter. Anyway, I thought you should know."

"Was Harlow okay? Did she seem hurt?"

Roman shrugs. "Finn didn't say otherwise."

"Thanks." My lip quivers. I'm in over my head. Underground. Trapped. I crumple to the ground like my bones are made of dried leaves. Roman reacts quickly.

"Here," he says, twisting the top off a container of water. "Drink."

I sit and gulp it down, and I feel almost instantly better. Dehydration, I say in my head. That's all this is. You were just thirsty and confused.

I return the water.

"I should go back now," he says.

"Wait," I say, though he hasn't moved. "The Hill's in trouble. We're . . . I need your help."

He reaches down and pulls me up. I don't look him in the eye, embarrassed for sounding desperate. Like Anouk, fragile and pathetic.

"Because of Harlow?"

"No." I shake my head. "Maybe; I don't know. There was an ambush when I was gone."

"Mainlanders?"

"How am I supposed to know? Boys, girls—they said something about the Colony leaving them no choice."

Roman covers his face. "That's not good."

"Obviously."

"No, it's *really* not good. The Colony's a secret, Wren. The Hill too. We're the only ones who know."

"*Used* to be the only ones."

Roman paces. "How'd they find out?"

"You're the one who said they were low on girls. What's that supposed to mean?"

"Something a Mainlander said last time we did a supply swap. He said girls were disappearing, snatched in the middle of the night. It didn't make much sense."

I think of Quinn's record—*Taken*.

"If you're the only ones who know about us, then it has be one of you who told. Someone in your village."

He stares at me pensively. "Or one of you."

I gasp. One of us. A Departed Girl. Someone had to have tipped them off. How else would they have known to use the Arrival Signal? It was the perfect way to lure the girls down to the beach.

Roman puts his hand up in a defensive position, and I realize I'm shining the flashlight directly into his eyes. I explain in detail the Arrival Signal, the empty boats. How we're all split up—the Mothers and Smalls in the woods, us in the cliff, and the rest of the girls stuck on the Hill under surveillance and told to pack. At the end of my account, he stares at me, perplexed. "You see a smoke signal offshore, and boats show up carrying babies?"

"Sometimes babies, sometimes supplies. Sometimes both. Depends on the color of the smoke."

He shakes his head. "The Colony never really explained that one."

I stare back at him. "They come from the old oil rig. How do *your* babies arrive? I suppose yours come by helicopter."

"No," he says, the puzzled look permanently on his face. "They usually come out of the medic's house when they're a few days old. With their parents." He stares at me with a look of bewilderment. "I think your Manual might be missing a few pages."

I have to turn around so he can't see my face. Even with my back to him, I cover my mouth, which is gaping open like the number zero. The perfect metaphor. I know nothing. None of us do. And how could we? We're isolated from the rest of the world. Ignorant.

"Listen," he says, grabbing my elbow. "I'll help you."

I gather myself. "This is crazy. Why should I trust you? I mean, I know I asked, but—"

"My mother," he says quietly. "You should trust me because of my mother."

"Why? What's a Mother got to do with this? What's so special about her?"

Roman places a hand on the back of his head.

"What's that supposed to mean?" I ask, frustration growing.

"The branding on your neck. *Colony*. She has it too."

CHAPTER 17

Section 5.6 – Things must never go back to the way they were. Your survival, all of humanity, depends on it.

I GRAB HIS arm. "Your mother's part of the Colony?"

He shakes his head. "No, she's part of the village."

"I don't get it."

"I don't either. Her stamp—you can't read it."

An invisible trickle of water echoes through the walls.

"Ever seen burnt skin?"

I shrug. "A few times." I recall an incident when a Small fell face-first into the fire and shudder. "If you can't read it, how do you know what it says?"

"I didn't—until I saw the back of your neck in the clearing. My mother just has a capital *C* and part of an *O*. The rest of it is scarred flesh. We're not allowed to talk about it. She's never cut her hair, but sometimes when she's welding, she ties it back and there it is, the scar, concealing all of her secrets."

I rub my forehead, exhausted, and step on my torch, killing what's left of the burning ember. "We should go back." I have nothing more to add, unable to process anything he's saying. I think of Quinn's analogy. I'm trying to swallow a whole deer, hooves, tail, and antlers. "We have a Mainlander."

"Like a prisoner?"

"Kind of. He's injured. He fell off the cliff."

Roman passes me his flashlight, and we exit through the same tunnel I entered from. The journey back seems quicker now that I know where I'm going. We go directly to the other tunnel and stop at the man's feet. Just behind him, Quinn, Blue, and Lennon are still asleep.

"Wren?" A morning whisper. I point the flashlight in Quinn's direction. She sits up and stretches her arms over her head. Roman steps back into the shadows.

"It's me."

She yawns and stands up. "My tailbone," she complains. Her eyes follow the beam of the flashlight to a spot on the ground. "What is that?" she asks. "Where did you get it?"

"A flashlight. Remember the one Nova found?"

"I know what a flashlight is."

"It's his." I light Roman from the knees-up.

"What's *he* doing here?" She charges, side-stepping around the body.

"He's going to help us."

"We don't need his help." The other girls, now awake but still on the ground, scramble to their feet. Their

154

legs, inevitably stiff from sleeping on the rock floor, look awkward. They move like broken puppets.

"He's one of them," Blue accuses.

"He's not." I shake my head. "He's an ally."

"An ally?" Quinn scoffs. She looks at Roman but stays put. "Is that why he almost broke your arm?"

Blue stares at me, silent and stunned. "Is that true?"

"Listen," I say, "he knows this place. Better than we do."

Quinn rolls her eyes. "Yeah?"

"He knew about these tunnels."

She takes a step back and bumps into the wall.

"He knows what happened to Harlow and he knows the Colony." I step over the body in front of me. His eyelids flutter.

"Where's Harlow?" Lennon asks.

"The Mainland. And you know how she got there?" I pause. "She took a helicopter."

"I told you I saw a helicopter," Blue throws her hands up indignantly. "No one believed me."

Blue studies Roman. "How do you know about the Colony?"

He screws his face into a grimace. "Let's just say we have an arrangement." He says nothing about his Mother.

"It doesn't matter," I say.

"It does matter." Quinn's teeth are gritted.

"What matters is that the Colony's been found out and, by extension, so has the Hill."

Lennon crosses her arms. "And that means what?"

"The Mainland's a mess," Roman starts.

"We got that, genius," Blue smirks. "'*The Mainland is overcrowded, hostile, and lawless.*' Section 2.0."

Roman presses his lips together. "You ever wonder why?"

Silence. The girls exchange curious glances. I think of Beck's map, the land more specks than masses, the ocean bleeding to the edges of the paper, endless.

"Too many people," Lennon offers.

"Kind of like right now." Quinn glares at Roman.

I flash her a cautionary glance.

Roman continues. "Too many people, yes, that's obvious. But do you understand why it's hostile?"

"There's not enough to go around." Blue's stomach growls on cue.

"Right. Resources are limited, but it goes back even further. Do you know why there's virtually nothing left? Why everyone's crowded on the Mainland?"

I want to raise my hand. I want to give the correct answer. I want him to applaud me for doing so, but I don't know. There's no validated story passed down from the girls before me. No intuitive spark of wisdom. Nothing to recite from the Manual. Only rumors.

Quinn clears her throat. "I hate to interrupt this titillating lesson, but *we know this already*. If you insist on wasting our time explaining life's most pressing mysteries, at least tell us something we don't know."

Roman turns his back on Quinn, isolating her from the circle.

"So, what then?" Lennon throws her head back in frustration. "Was it a flood? A disease—?"

"That's not the point," Roman cuts her off.

"You don't have a point," Quinn retorts, her voice louder than before, bouncing off the cave walls at a menacing pitch. I flinch. She muscles her way back into the circle.

"The Colony blames males for destroying the Earth," Roman says.

Lennon scrunches her face. "Huh?"

"That won't mean much if you don't know the way things used to be."

"Boys ruined the earth?" Blue asks.

"According to the Colony, they did," Roman exhales.

The tunnel fades into quiet contemplation. I stare at the ground. A piece of ornamental fruit from an American bittersweet shrub, red and lopsided, rests at my feet. I bend to pick it up, cupping it my hand carefully so as not to squish it. "Well, did they?" I ask. "*Did* men destroy the Earth?"

We all stare at Roman. He shifts and fidgets with his backpack as if it suddenly weighs a thousand pounds. Then he tosses his hair from his eyes.

"We're all responsible. For taking more than we need. Not looking after the environment. Thinking only of ourselves."

"That doesn't explain the blame."

"Traditionally, men have made most of the decisions. That's why the Colony started. The women wanted to be in charge—exclusively. To start over, and more importantly, to prevent it from happening again."

Quinn rolls her eyes. "So even if it is their fault, that still doesn't explain why a bunch of Mainlanders would show up here." She faces Blue and Lennon. "You know what the Hill is? It's a garbage dump."

Blue's expression changes. Lennon tilts her head.

"You have something they don't," Roman explains.

"Ha!" Quinn scoffs. "Like what? Is it our stockpile of dead batteries? Rusted car parts? Soiled sheets? Three-legged chairs? Our beloved crickets?"

"No," he says matter-of-factly. "What you have is skill. The Colony"—he shakes his head, awe in his eyes—"is *thriving*. The women have figured out how to rebuild. From nothing. They work together. You're part of that. But most of the Mainland . . ." He winces at the thought. "It's desperate. Lawless. People are hungry. They're becoming feral. They don't know what or how to do anything. They care only about the next meal, where they're going to sleep for the night, who they need to kill to make it happen."

"They want *us*," Lennon says, equal parts impressed and horrified.

"So what we are we supposed to do?" Quinn asks, still irritated.

"Keep your fingers crossed that it's just this small group of bandits who knows."

"We need to kill them," Lennon says. "They can't go back alive."

Blue smirks. "There are only four of us."

"Five," Roman says.

"We need a plan." I lean against the wall, dizzy. "But first I have to eat."

The girls agree, touching their stomachs, and the conversation goes quiet. "Quinn, why don't you three search for food?"

She shoots me a look, then grabs the back of my arm. "I have to show you something," she says, leading me away from the group. When we're a safe distance away, she lets go of my arm and stomps her foot childishly. "I'm not leaving you two alone."

"Why not?"

"Because you're planning things without me."

"We haven't planned a thing. He only came here because he had information about Harlow."

"Then why hasn't he left?"

"Because I asked him to stay."

"You *asked* him?" Her eyes blaze.

I throw up my arms in frustration.

"You didn't even consult me."

"Just yesterday, you accused me of making stupid, naive decisions."

"And you still are," she says, shoulders slumped.

"Because I'm enlisting help from the one person around here who seems to know more than us? How is that naive? Naive is continuing to believe the Manual has all the answers. Naive is thinking we can do this on our own. It's denying help when we need it. We're outnumbered!"

"Naive is thinking you cared about me."

Not again. "Why do you have to keep making this personal? You know I care about you. You're my best friend. That's why I'm trying to make decisions that'll get us through this. Together."

Quinn looks away, eyes glassy. She kicks at a rock, and we both watch it skip haphazardly across the ground.

"Excuse me?" Lennon says, returning my knife. "The big guy's dead."

Quinn and I lock eyes. "Please, Quinn. I'm begging. I know I've made some mistakes. You don't have to trust Roman. But—please. Trust me."

CHAPTER 18

Section 5.7 – Accountability lies with those who hold power and execute policy.

I RUSH BACK to the group, leaving Quinn to sulk on the wall. Roman and Blue are on their knees, flanking the man's wide shoulders.

"I can't get a pulse," Roman says.

The man's eyes are partially open. I bend down to examine them, hoping for even the tiniest hint of life, any sign that his cells are fighting to exist for one more day, one more minute, one more second. But he's gone. I see nothing but my reflection, patched and bent. I look crippled. Roman gently pulls me off him. Quinn arrives and stands at his feet. No one comments.

"We're going to get some food," Quinn finally says, gesturing for the others to join her.

I watch them leave through the tunnel. Roman starts going through the man's pockets. I'm disturbed. "What are you doing?"

"He might have clues on him," he says, rifling through a wad of papers. "Or something we can use."

"But he only just died. Seconds ago."

He looks at me considerably less sensitively than he did only minutes before. "I know it's hard, Wren, but you have to decide what's important. You have no idea what type of danger you're in, and he might have information that can help."

Roman reaches into the man's pants pocket and pulls out a square object that he opens like a book.

"Emmett James Titterton," he says. "That's a mouthful."

"What is it?"

"His wallet. And this is his driver's license." He flips the open wallet around to face me, exposing a card that displays the man's photograph. "Not that there are any drivable roads left on the Mainland. He'd get further on a bike."

"Emmett," I say out loud. Knowing his name makes his death seem more tragic. "What do we do with him?"

"We should probably take him back to the beach. Won't be long before he starts to rot." He sniffs. "These tunnels smell bad enough without a decomposing body to add to the mix." He tosses the wallet aside and continues to go through the contents of his pockets. I pick up the wallet and stare at his picture again. There are more cards inside a row of slits, but they don't have any photographs, and I have no idea what they're for. "A phone," Roman says, holding a device I assume he's pulled out of a back pocket, based on the position of Emmett's body.

"That's probably what was making noise this morning." I don't tell him I have no clue how it works, but he seems to know this and explains.

"You use it to talk to people."

"Like a radio?"

"Kind of," he says. "How do you think we communicate with the Colony?"

The Colony has a *phone*? We're using handwritten messages and flares and Departing Girls . . . I stop. Of course. I'm reminded of my Mother's words: *The Manual is big because we have to learn how to do everything.*

"Some others on the Mainland have them," Roman continues, "but they rarely work around here. They need towers to connect to, and we only have a few."

"I know. I climbed one."

He tucks the device in his pocket and picks up the flashlight, which he's strategically placed on top of Quinn's pack for optimum light. "I'm going to get more water," he says.

"I don't have any light."

He pulls the device back out of his pocket and flips a switch on the side, causing it to emit a glow brighter than his own flashlight. "Use this," he says. "I'll meet you outside the entrance of the cliff in a bit. We can move him later."

I turn the glowing phone around in my hands, lighting up random parts of the tunnel. Before he leaves, he extends me his hand; I'm still kneeling beside Emmett's body. I take his wrist. We face each other in the artificial light. I swallow what feels like thunder rolling up from my chest. Anticipation. Except I have no idea what I'm anticipating. I can't imagine anything he could say or do that warrants what feels like a million birds flapping inside my rib cage.

Then he reaches over and runs the back of his hand down my cheek. It feels lovely, not threatening. I try to hush myself, aware that my breathing has become loud and erratic. I exhale as he tucks a piece of my hair behind my ear, his fingertips grazing the side of my neck only long enough that I can feel it, and then his arm simply drops by his side, and he turns to go.

I say nothing but feel a tremendous release, as though the millions of birds trapped inside my chest have just been set free. I can't stop smiling.

When the moment passes, I feel infused with energy. I look through my pack for traces of food, and when I find nothing, I equip my pockets with my knife and the glowing phone. Before I leave to find the others, I place Emmett's wallet back in his pocket and cover him with a shirt.

But when I turn to go, Quinn is there.

SHE STANDS TEN feet away, her torch barely lit, as though the oxygen has become scarce. She balances a stack of mussels in the crook of her arm. Before I can tell her how relieved I am to see food, she says, "You like him."

How long was she standing there? Did she see the way he touched my face? Stop smiling, I command myself.

"He's helpful." I can't look her in the eye.

"Not like that," she says. "You act different around him."

"Because he's a stranger," I argue. "Of course I'm going to act different. I don't entirely trust him yet."

"That's not what I mean," she says. "It's like you *want* to be around him."

She's right. Quinn has put into words exactly what I haven't. I want to be around him.

"That's not true. I just want to learn from him. I want to know what he knows. I think we'll all be better off if we have a greater understanding of what's going on around us."

"Is that all?"

"What is this?" My ears are hot with resentment.

"What?" Her tone implies I'm overreacting. I likely am.

I exhale discreetly and make a conscious effort to present an expression of calm. "It just feels like an inquisition."

Quinn stares. "An inquisition for you," she says quietly. "For me, a betrayal."

"No one's betraying anyone. Me talking to him doesn't change us. Here." I offer her the phone. "Trade."

She agrees to the exchange, handing me her dying torch.

"I need you to lead us out." She rejects my attempt to link arms and quickens her pace, leaving me a few steps behind. Neither of us speaks.

When we emerge from the crack in the cliff, Blue and Lennon are huddled over a small fire they've constructed from debris and driftwood. Empty shells litter the space around them. There is also a small pile of nuts assembled in the shape of a pyramid.

"We collected those yesterday," Blue says. She takes a nut from the top, causing the pyramid to collapse. Quinn squats down and drops the mussels beside the fire. There is no sign of Roman.

Lennon passes me a mixture of nuts, shellfish, and greens on a piece of bark with a depression in the middle, like a shallow bowl. The fish is unevenly cooked—equal parts charred and wet, but the nourishment and fresh air are fulfilling.

I look at the smoke drifting in upward spirals from the fire and wonder if it will draw attention to our location. Quinn follows my gaze and reads my mind.

"They won't be able to see," she says. "The smoke is gone before it can crest over the cliff."

"They might smell it."

"We're done, anyway." Blue crushes what remains of the fire with a rock.

"What's the plan?" Quinn looks eager, in need of a distraction.

"Surveillance," I reply. "We need to know how many there are and where they're positioned. Whether they're armed. Ideally, we'll also make contact with Clover, so she knows we're here."

"Are we splitting up?" Quinn asks, gripping the phone.

"There's only one way to the beach. We'll stay together until we reach it and decide from there."

"There's another way," Roman pipes up from behind us. His voice makes me jump. He wipes sweat from his forehead. "Through the cliff, there's another tunnel. Takes you right out to the woods alongside the path that runs up and down your Hill."

"I'll go with you," Quinn volunteers.

I stare at her sharply.

"It's a bit of a climb," Roman warns.

"Good," she says. "Climbing's my thing." She passes Roman the phone.

"Your hand," I remind her.

"It's better."

"Fine." I try to sound nonchalant, like I don't know exactly what she's doing—trying to make me jealous, which is exactly how I feel. I want to go with him. Desperately. But maybe this is a good thing, a chance for things to cool. "Blue, Lennon, and I will go this way." I use my knife as a pointer. "And you two can take the tunnel." I face away from Roman because I'm inexplicably mad at him.

He reaches for my elbow. "And from there, what?"

I pull my arm away. "Depends."

He exhales, and I hear him turn. His footsteps start heavy but grow faint as he distances himself.

Quinn calls after him, "Wait up."

I turn around only to see both of them slip into the crack in the cliff.

"Let's go."

Lennon nods, wiping remnants of fish from her face. A complicated braid dangles over her shoulder. I don't know where she found the time to weave it.

"I don't have a weapon," Blue says.

"I have my knife."

"There are three of us."

I search our surroundings. "Can you make something? A spear? A club?"

Lennon wanders off toward the cliff.

"Got any string?" Blue asks.

I think of Emmett's complicated backpack. "I can get you some." I hand off the knife to Lennon. "I'll be right back," I say, slipping into the tunnel. I parade through the darkness unlit until I sense the fork ahead. I listen for Quinn and Roman, but the underground is still, its mouth zipped shut.

I flick the lighter on, illuminating the grisly scene: the generous dead body, a random mussel. A mouse darts across, springboarding over Emmett's bloated stomach, and disappears with a faint squeak. Silence again.

"Hell," I exhale, adrenaline coursing through my legs.

I have to flip him over to access his backpack. I put the lighter in my pocket, squat beside him, and decide to roll him towards me. I wedge my hands under the massive expanse of his back and heave, grunting at the task. It takes three tries before I muscle the right amount of force to turn him over, duckwalking backward so he doesn't collapse on top of me.

I maneuver myself onto my knees, depress the switch on the lighter, and memorize the position of the straps before the light goes out. I yank each strap alternately until the backpack is freed, and I stand.

"Sorry, Emmett," I say. "You shouldn't have been on our beach. You should never have come to the Hill." I feel my way out of the tunnel, dragging the backpack behind me, not sure what kind of bodily fluids it might have soaked up. It takes a good minute for my eye to adjust when I exit the crack. In my short absence, Lennon and Blue have made quick work.

"Check it out," Lennon says, turning a wooden spear in her hands, the tip whittled to perfection, so the point is nearly invisible.

"Got that string?" Blue holds a rock and a stick.

"A club," I say, putting the pieces together.

She nods.

I take my knife back from Lennon and begin severing the stretchy cords dangling from the backpack. Blue starts fastening the rock to the end of the stick, winding the cordage with rapid flicks of her wrist to secure the weapon. I smile, satisfied. The luck of getting stuck with two ingenious Hunters. It makes up for losing Quinn, for losing Roman.

"There's not enough," Blue determines, giving the club a mild shake, the rock shifting and nearly falling. "You got anything else?"

"You can take the string from my pack."

She agrees, accepting the knife and cutting the string that keeps the mouth of my bag cinched together.

"You almost done?" I ask Blue. "I don't know how long it'll take for Quinn and Roman to go through the tunnel. They could already be out the other side, waiting."

Blue holds up the finished club, eyes dancing. "Now I'm ready."

"Beautiful. A work of art. Or death." I stick my knife in my pocket. "I'll clean up here and catch up."

Blue leads, and they disappear around the corner. A seagull bobs just offshore. I ferry the remains of the morning fire into the ocean and then roll my pack in a way that things won't fall out, despite the gaping hole at the top.

Emmett's backpack sits upright beside me, a grave marker, a tombstone. I snatch it, place it between my legs and unzip the main compartment, dumping everything onto the ground. A tackle box of fishing lures tumbles out. A compass, the glass foggy and cracked, falls out, along with a hat. A bruised apple rolls out from the bottom. Something is stuck. I peel open the sides of the bag, avoiding the bloodstains marring the gray fabric. A book is wedged inside. I gingerly free it from the lining and yank it out. The title makes me choke.

The Manual.

I flip through madly, catching bits of text: *tourniquet, ligament strain, sheet knot, wickiup, teething, scat key*. I study the bottom of each page, searching for the COLONY stamp. It's there in faded black. I frantically whip the pages back to the beginning. The title page is also in faded black, the table of contents not in color. It's a copy. Section 1.0.

I spread the book across my knees and finger-read each line, the type sterile and serious.

It was not because of a plague. There was no Black Death or Ebola. No COVID-19, 30, or 41. No antibiotic-resistant virus that swept the earth. Nor was it a single act of nature. There was no asteroid, no "big one," no biblical flood, no Category 5 hurricane named after your mother. There was no World War III or V or XVII. No one pushed the notorious red button. And it was not because the world was taken over by a hoard of war-mongering robots. It wasn't artificial intelligence. Alexa had nothing to do with it.

It was them. They did it. Gradually ... over time. Like the slow death of a coral reef, a clean river, an entire species.

They overfished. Overfarmed. Overlogged. Overmined. Overindulged. Overconsumed. Overdrilled. Because they always wanted more.

They practiced slavery. They practiced torture. They practiced genocide. They practiced rape. They turned boys into soldiers, girls into wives. They constructed race and gender and institutions to uphold them.

They cheered cockfights and dogfights and

bullfights. They turned animals into commodities. Snatched away babies with their eyes still closed, so they were unable to discern where their mothers had gone. They put them in isolation. They put them in zoos, in stalls, in cells, and factory farms. They killed them for pleasure, killed them for lust. Sometimes they killed them for no reason at all.

They invented sarin gas and napalm and Agent Orange. BPA, CFCs, DDT.

They made heavy water, Kalashnikovs, plastics that filled the bellies of whales and choked the necks of turtles.

I pause. I've seen turtles like that.

They loved guns and coal and yachts. They spilled champagne on their suits, oil in the rivers, blood through the streets.

No, it was not an act of God or science or nature. It was a long, drawn-out act of MEN.

I stare at the page. What is napalm? What is a Kalashnikov? Champagne? Heavy water? The cover falls shut, and I look out at the ocean, unassuming but never-ending. I can't imagine these things that men did. And why one was carrying our secrets on his back.

There's no time for contemplation. Hands trembling,

I shove the Manual into my pack, re-roll the opening, and set out to catch up with Lennon and Blue. The tide is in, and I have to get wet to circumnavigate a portion of the cliff. I charge into the ocean, knee-deep, my expression steadfast, though the temperature kidnaps my breath. I need to get back to the Hill. My fists clench. There will be blood.

CHAPTER 19

Section 9.3 – ... effective non-choke options
include joint manipulation, limb strangu-
lation, and pain submissions.

THEY WAIT BY the part of the cliff where Quinn and
I jumped off. The water is only ankle-deep. For now, I
keep the Manual hidden. I don't tell them about Section
1.0 and the Colony's origins. Roman pretty much had it
right.

We travel in single file. From this angle, we are
detectable only if someone is in the water. The cliff gets
shorter as we get closer, eventually stopping at chest
height. We walk hunched over until it ceases altogether,
curving right where it flanks the beach, the Hill.

I gesture for the girls to get down lower as I peer
around the corner. Three boats are jammed up against
the opening of the cave, one of them upside down. A
fourth boat, tethered, bobs within feet of the shoreline,
tacking side to side with each wave. I lean in further to
get a view of the path and see two boys. One is sitting
barefoot, smacking the soles of his shoes together, as if

removing sand from the insides. The other just stands there. I report this to Lennon and Blue.

"What exactly are they doing?" Lennon repositions herself for a better view.

"Nothing, really."

"Are they armed?" Blue asks. I conceal myself behind the cliff and inhale a brave breath before taking a second look. The barefoot boy puts his shoes back on and stands. The other one picks up a rock and throws it with a technique that suggests the rock will skip, but it doesn't. It's too big. I can tell from the resounding *plunk*.

"What was that?" Lennon asks.

"They're trying to skip rocks." The other boy has joined in. His second attempt is successful and a rock darts across the water, reappearing three times before it vanishes.

"Shouldn't they be doing something?"

"Better they're down here skipping rocks than up there."

"But we can't do anything until they're off the beach."

"I don't think they're going anywhere." Another rock whizzes across the water. "They've probably been assigned to guard it."

"So what, are we just going to stay here until they go to sleep? I can't stand like this for much longer," Lennon complains.

"You can't stand, but you can swim, right? That's how you escaped."

Her eyebrows shift like she doesn't know where I'm going with the question.

"To that boat." I point to the only one in the water.

"And you don't think they're going to see me swim to it?"

"Not if you swim underwater."

She bites her nails, assessing the distance.

"It's no further than what you did before," I say. "I'll go first."

"I can't swim that." Blue shakes her head. "Not underwater, anyway. I can't hold my breath that long."

"Then you stay here." I remove my pack, make sure it's secure, and pass it to her. "We'll swim over."

"And then what?" Lennon asks.

"We'll fight them."

"How?" Blue pins my pack against the rock as the sea laps at our feet.

"Jiujitsu. It's the one thing the Colony got right."

"Quinn said Roman arm-barred you."

"He did. But I took *him* down, and I almost choked him. It was a fair fight."

"And what if they fight back? What if they kill us?"

I remove my boots. "Then we'll be dead." I take a quick look to see where the boys are positioned. A rock dances past and slices into the water a few feet away. I take a huge breath, align myself with the boat, and dive in, careful to enter the water out of view. My underwater glides are powerful, like I'm peeling away the water with each stroke. I guess long arms are handy for swimming.

I can't open my eyes. After what seems close to a minute, my fingertips graze a rope. I grab onto it with

176

both hands. My oxygen supply is low, but I resist sur-facing in case I come up on the wrong side of the boat in full view. Instead, I position myself underneath it and come up for air, finding the shallow space where the boat's sides curve up from its bottom. I gently push away and bring my head to the surface, relieved that I'm on the correct side, out of the boys' view. I use the rope to pull myself to the end, stick my forearm up out of the water, and wave for Lennon to join me. She plugs her nose and dives in. I immediately panic. She won't make the distance if she's only using one arm to swim.

"Come on," I urge. She glides only a few inches below the surface. Slowly. About ten feet from the rope, which I'm still clinging to maintain my footing on the ocean floor, she starts to surface. "Stay down," I say, but she doesn't stay down.

She rolls from her front to her back and comes out of the water, gasping for air. Her hair, which must have come loose from its braid, spreads across her face, dark like seaweed but fine like jellyfish tentacles. I hear com-motion on the beach. I catch a glimpse of the boys, who are now standing on the water's edge, pointing in our direction. Across the way, Blue is covering her mouth, which confirms my fear that Lennon has been spotted.

I half-swim, half-walk around the boat. "Hurry up."

She rolls back onto her stomach again and takes a messy breath that I'm sure is comprised mostly of water before collapsing below the surface. I go underwater too, swimming toward her with my hands outstretched. I pull her first by her hair, which feels wrong until I can secure the neck of her shirt in my fist. When we get to the other side of the boat, I pull her to the surface.

Lennon emerges, dizzy and disoriented. Drool drips from her chin, a spring thaw. She wipes it away, gets bumped by a breaking wave and falls into me. I push her back up by her shoulders and steady her in the water.

"Are you okay?" I ask, irritated that she volunteered to swim when she was clearly incapable.

She coughs and cries and nods her head. "I swallowed a lot of water."

A rock zips towards us and hits the boat, plunking into the sea.

"That was not a skipping rock," I say, marveling at the speed in which it was thrown.

"They're trying to hit us." Lennon flaps her arms, helpless.

I dive under the water and find the rock, which is heavy enough it drags me down, and then I throw it back to the beach. It hits one of the boys in the leg. He cradles his knee, lifting it towards his chest. I watch him bend and straighten it several times before he empties his pockets and charges into the water. I don't wait for him.

"Get to the shore," I say, without turning around. "Go to the cave."

"But—"

I ignore her and run toward the boy. Despite the fact that I'm in deeper water, I move faster than him, and for a split second, he hesitates. I take him down, lunging low into his legs. It's not graceful, and we both go under the water. I scramble below the surface, but as I'm about to come up for air, his hand wraps around my face like a paw and holds me down. I clamp my hands around his wrist and twist it until he releases my face and howls.

"You're going to break it!"

"I could." More like dislocate his elbow. But I don't. He whimpers like a baby. A trapped animal. Injured but alive, conceding control. "I'm not going to break your arm," I say, "even though you tried to kill me with that rock."

"Who are you?" His words barely make it through his gritted teeth.

"A mermaid." I smile, though he can't see because he's facedown, a few inches above the water. "Where did your friend go?"

"He went for backup."

"How many of you are there?"

"Twelve."

I pull his arm up an inch, like a lever. The amount is almost negligible, but he cries out in pain. "Why are you here?"

"I just answered a call," he spits.

"A call for what?"

"Crew members." He turns his face. It's covered in pain.

"For what purpose?"

He groans. "Retaliation."

"Retaliation?" A wave nearly topples us over. What could possibly be happening on the Mainland?

"Against the Colony." His breath catches as he tries to straighten.

"And what did the Colony ever do to you?"

He whispers, "Nothing. That's the whole point. It's done absolutely nothing to help anyone outside of it. People are dying; they have medicine, but they won't provide it. People are hungry; they have food, but they won't share it. People need skills; they have you, but they won't—"

I release his arm, which flops down like it's dead. A gutted fish. Then I place my fingertip under his chin and guide him up, so we're standing face-to-face.

When I go to speak, though, I lose my breath. It feels like I've swallowed my words. His own mouth gapes open like the cave behind him.

Out of my periphery, I notice Lennon has made it ashore. She is on all fours, her back heaving up and down like she just swam from the Mainland. I try again to speak to the boy in front of me—to order him to cancel the backup, to tell the rest of them it was all a mistake, but the words refuse to float to the surface. Instead, I stare into his pigeon-gray eyes and the band of freckles that stretches across his cheekbones like a constellation. His thin upper lip, long arms. I open my mouth to speak, but he says it first.

"You look just like me."

CHAPTER 20

Section 6.4 – Some plant species are toxic and should not be consumed. Refer to Appendix D: POISONOUS PLANTS

BEFORE I CAN reply, I hear footsteps bearing down on the path to the beach.

"Get down," he says.

I duck below the surface of the water, unsure whether to swim or freeze. I can't hear or see what's going on. I count to ten, twenty, fifty. When I reach a minute, panic sets in. My lungs feel squeezed, like they might collapse. I exhale a tiny fraction of the breath I've been able to hold, but it's a slippery slope, and within seconds, I've let my entire breath go. An explosion of bubbles gallops to the surface, and then I'm pulled out of the water.

The beach is empty. "Where'd they go?"

"Back up the hill." He looks over his shoulder. There's a mark behind his ear, a tiny black *X*. "I told them it was a false alarm."

I'm embarrassed by the way I stagger to shore, my legs crisscrossing and stumbling like I've never used them before. The boy picks up on this. "Guess you should have stuck with your tail," he says, referring to my comment about being a mermaid.

I ignore him. "What's your name?"

"Abbott."

I head toward the cave, where our voices are less likely to carry. "Why do you look like me?"

"You wear a patch."

"What's that have to do with anything?"

Lennon is curled up in the fetal position, whimpering.

"Get up," I tell her. "You're not going to scare anyone off acting like that."

She stops crying and pulls herself to a seated position. She looks up at me, big-eyed, then at Abbott. Her expression changes. She sees it too. The resemblance.

"I don't know," I say before she has a chance to ask the question. "We just do."

In the distance, Blue makes her way through the water, chest-deep, carrying all of our belongings over her head. Before she reaches the shore, Quinn slips into the cave seemingly out of nowhere and crashes heavily against the wall. She's out of breath.

"Where's Roman?" I ask.

"I told him we didn't need him."

"What do you mean, you told him we didn't need him?"

"I explained that we no longer required his services and to have a nice day."

"Why would you do that?"

"Because we don't need him."

"You're unbelievable." *Insubordinate.* I want to shake her. "Where did he go?"

"He went home, where he belongs."

I step out of the cave and look toward the forest. Nothing. No one. I return to face Quinn. "I decide if we need someone. Not you."

Abbott shifts uncomfortably from one foot to the other.

"Looks like you've already found a replacement," she sneers.

"A prisoner."

Quinn looks at Abbott contemplatively, like he's a meal and she's trying to decide how she'll prepare him. Then her eyes dart from him to me, as though we're passing an invisible ball between us and she's trying to keep track. She doesn't say anything, but her expression changes from contempt to wonder.

I turn my back on her. "How are you organized?"

Out of a raised chin, Abbott says, "We're all over."

I get in his face. "Are you getting cocky?"

He crosses his arms over his chest.

"Be more specific."

"That's it," he says. "We're all over the place."

I plead with my eye for him to cooperate, so I don't have to set an example of him. But it's like looking in a mirror.

"Who brought you here?"

"Emmett."

"Stocky, with dark, curly hair?" I nod toward Quinn. "Like hers?"

His eyes shift between Quinn and me. He nods.

"You know where he is?" I ask.

Abbott shakes his head.

"He's dead," Quinn says.

Abbott looks at me for confirmation, unsure whether to believe Quinn, who, after little sleep, looks like she's crawled out of a hole in the ground.

"They're scattered all over," he says again.

"Armed?"

"Some of them."

I feel for my knife, run my fingertips along the length of the handle, and leave the cave, tossing sand behind me with each step.

"Where are you going?" Quinn asks.

I don't turn around. "Up."

"Without a plan?"

"The plan is to go up, and we take them out one at a time. Hand to hand."

Quinn catches me stride for stride. "One on one?"

At my feet is a lump of seaweed. I scoop it up and thrust it toward the water, and it hits the surface with an audible smack, like a slap in the face. "Two on one."

I wipe my wet hands on my shirt and call back to Lennon, "You stay here and guard him."

She nods, bright-eyed and enthusiastic. Though she's quick and agile, she doesn't love combat. Bit of an Assignment fail. She should have been a Mother or a Supplier. Anything but a Hunter.

"What about me?" Blue asks, gripping the club.

"You're in charge of the beach. Just as they were. Defend it."

The possibility of a fight appeases her, and she starts yanking on a branch from a dead tree that hangs over the cave like a canopy. She'll manage to turn it into something deadly to go with the club.

I head toward the path that leads uphill, but come to an abrupt stop when something offshore catches my eye.

"What?" Quinn says.

"You lead." I grab her arm and swing her body in front of mine, like an aggressive grappling partner.

She looks at me suspiciously, so I follow up with an affirming shove between her shoulder blades, and she keeps moving. When she's a few paces ahead, I look back toward the cliff, where it flanks the water. Roman climbs up the side, muscling his way to the top with ease, like he's done it a thousand times. At the top, he looks back toward the beach. I think we make eye contact, but it's too far to be certain. Ahead of me, Quinn stops, sensing I've lagged behind. I speed up until she resumes the trek uphill. When I know she's not looking, I lift my hand to wave. Roman waves back, and my mouth erupts into a cheek-pulling smile that I can't contain.

We tread up the path alongside the forest, and I focus on keeping a neutral expression on my face. When the path deviates toward the Hill, Quinn pulls me off to the side. I wonder if she's seen something I missed.

"Why are you smiling?"

"I'm not."

"You are. What's so funny? What could possibly be amusing right now?"

"Nothing." I bite my lip. "Why are we here?"

"Because of *that*." She points toward a small opening in a rock. "That's where the tunnel comes out."

I stare at the partially concealed hole. It doesn't look big enough for my arm. "How did you fit through that?"

"The left side can be pushed open." She nudges it with her knee. "That piece is not attached."

It resembles a small tomb. A rabbit burrow. Quinn, seeming to sense movement somewhere, pulls me to the side. We take cover behind the trunk of a huge tree, though I can't see anyone.

She whispers, "Are we seriously doing this? Just you and me?"

Isn't that what you want? "We have to."

"What if we fail?"

"What if we win?"

"We're outnumbered, Wren. And we've barely eaten."

"We have nothing to lose."

Her eyes bulge. "The Hill."

"We've already lost it, Quinn. The minute they stepped foot on the beach. All we can do now is try to take it back."

"They might kill us."

"They might. But I'd rather die trying than let them keep it."

Quinn opens and closes her damaged hand. "Thought you no longer believed in the Colony?"

"I said I have a hard time trusting them. That's different."

"But you're willing to die for it?"

I shake my head. "I'm willing to die for the Hill."

Her eyes widen.

"Come on, Quinn. Just the other day you complained about our entire training going to waste because we have no reason to use it. But maybe this is it. What if everything we've ever done—every takedown, every shot, every hill sprint, every dig, every cricket—what if it all comes down to this very moment?"

Quinn nods and starts to pace. "You're right," she says. "You're absolutely right. Let's go. Let's do this."

I smile at the fierceness in her eyes, the bravery in her shoulders, the loyalty in her heart. She would die for the Hill. She would die for me.

Quinn takes a deep breath and gets to work. She surveys the scene beyond the tree, stretching her neck.

"Anything?"

"Clear."

"Let's keep going."

We continue uphill through the forest, parallel to the path. Less than a week ago, we'd never have imagined breaking such a deliberate and dangerous rule.

Midway up, we find a drape of fabric—a flag—attached to the branch of a tree. It's one we tied when we left to find Harlow. From this vantage point, we see the girls, some of them with their mouths and hands bound, others on their knees, excavating a steep swath of hill, where the Westside and Eastside Forests collide. Boys and two girls surround them.

I drop to my knees, nauseated with fear, the threat real. Only one of them has a visible weapon—a rifle— slung over his shoulder, the kind described in the Manual, a slick combination of cool metal and polished wood, the barrel impossibly long. We watch breathlessly for a few minutes until the girls all stand, as though commanded. Then, as a group, they descend the Hill in our direction. About twenty paces down, a boy hollers, "Stop." The girls obey. "Dig," he commands. For what purpose?

A Collector has a black eye. Another limps. One of the enemy girls, blond and wiry, pushes a Hunter to the ground and laughs.

"I don't understand this," Quinn says. "They look so weak. There's no fight."

"What do you expect? He has a gun."

"The girls, then. They could take them on."

"Not tied up they can't, and not as long as he's armed." I gesture toward Rifle Boy.

"But look how scrawny some of them are."

"He. Has. A. Gun," I repeat, loud and slow so the words might stick.

Quinn draws back. "What are we going to do?"

Before I have a chance to answer, Clover, who's working on her knees, lets out a high-pitched scream, like she's been impaled. We both jump. She drops the trowel she's been using and grabs onto her wrist. Even from a distance, we see her body tremble.

"What happened?"

I strain my eye. "I don't know, but I see blood."

Quinn moves to the edge of the forest for a better view. I follow behind, picking my way through the branches.

A few boys gather around Clover. Rifle Boy crouches down to look at her wrist. I imagine he tells her to keep working, because she positions herself back on her knees and picks up the trowel.

"This is ridiculous." I scan the hillside and tally the number of boys. "I only count seven. And the two girls. Nine."

"Eleven," Quinn says. She rests her chin on my shoulder so that our cheekbones are pressed together and then points in two directions, where additional boys stand guard.

Across from us, we watch a shirtless boy, pale as winter, shove his crotch in a Forager's face, a band of fabric binding her mouth. "Check it," he says. "Want a little piece?"

A boy laughs. Another asks, "You like that?"

I rise.

"What are they doing?" Quinn asks.

The Forager turns her face to the side. The blonde enemy girl shifts uncomfortably. "Knock it off," she tells the offending boy.

He looks at her. "You jealous? You want some?"

"I want to kill him," I mutter. I want to wrap my hands around his neck and push my thumbs so deep into his throat you can see the indents from the other side.

"There's *eleven* of them," Quinn says.

I take my knife out of my pocket.

"Wait." Quinn grabs my arm. "We should take the guards out first. Ambush them from behind."

She's right. As guards, they're likely armed. Adrenaline rushes through my body, making my legs feel equal parts weak and mythically strong. I bear-walk a few paces higher, trying to keep pace.

"Psst," Quinn calls out.

I stay hunched and look for her. She's moved deeper into the woods but continues to climb with lithe swiftness. She beckons for me to follow, and I watch her move three trees forward, stealthily shifting between them. Hide-and-seek. We are midway between the edge of the scene and the first guard. I catch up to Quinn, lacking her finesse as I stumble over a bush, but before I have a chance to steady myself, she pushes forward again, arcing to the left.

She whispers, "I got him," placing her spear on the ground.

I hold my breath as she closes in behind the first guard. He is slightly shorter than her, but thick. His hair is mostly shorn, but dark as a shadow. They are face-to-face for only a second before she tackles him, an inside leg trip, and stomps on his neck. I shudder.

The rest of the boys and the two girls assemble into a semi-circle around Rifle Boy. No one seems to notice the guard is missing, or no one cares. They argue about something. Emmett's name is tossed around. They don't seem to know what to do without him. They have no idea he's dead.

Rifle Boy then turns from the group. "We're hungry," he announces, a hand spread across his stomach. "Let's eat." The girls disperse.

When I reach Quinn, the guard is unconscious. Blood trickles from his ear.

"What are they doing?" Her face is red and sweaty, eyes menacing.

"Stopping to eat. This is our chance."

"What do I do with him?" She fixes her shirt, which is twisted, and tucks her hair behind her ears. Seconds later, it springs forward.

"Leave him."

The boys depart in a group and head up toward the Quarters. We follow, taking the long way through the trees until we find an adequate place to spy. The boys lounge. The girls cook, including theirs.

"Are they preparing their food?"

"Looks like it," Quinn says.

I twitch. Clover holds her wrist while everyone capable of moving shuffles around, scrounging for food. I watch a Hunter scoot downhill, hands bound. She finds a rock and awkwardly goes to work on the cloth keeping her wrists tied.

"I have an idea."

"Now what?"

"Canary peas."

Quinn's stare is blank, like I've spoken another language. "What the hell are canary peas?"

"These." I gesture with my foot toward a clump of plants to the side of us. The leaves are moth-brown and canoe-shaped. They look dead but cradle seeds that are brighter and redder than anything else in our natural world—not the color you'd expect, given the name. The ends of the seeds are black, as though they were dipped in tar. Ladybugs without spots.

"Those," Quinn says. "They make people go crazy."

"They can also kill you."

CHAPTER 21

Section 9.2 – Guerrilla warfare may include sabotage, deception, raids, petty warfare, ambushes, and other tactics performed by a small group of combatants.

QUINN AND I harvest handfuls of seeds, removing them with sticks onto a piece of cloth, so our skin never makes direct contact. I take a second to revel in their beauty before I fold in the corners of the fabric to create a pouch.

"How do we get them over there?"

"We wait until one of the girls comes into the woods."

Quinn considers this. A Forager will likely venture in, searching for fresh herbs or kindling. We sit in contemplative silence for what seems like an hour, but no one leaves the meal area.

"We're running out of time." She drums her healthy fingers on the ground, the others still loosely bound in a mock cast. "No one's coming."

"I have an idea," I whisper. "I'll take them over myself."

"You're going to take them over? Good luck not getting shot."

I don't wait for her approval. I step out of the forest and onto the Hill, passing the swath of land that was excavated only minutes ago. Bits of trash poke out from the surface like tombstones. The seeds stain the pouch pink as I walk, as though they're bleeding.

The boys laze a safe distance from the cooking fire. The blond stands somewhere in between. Another girl sits on one of the boy's laps—purposely, it seems. At one point, he tilts her chin and kisses her. I stumble, confused but enthralled. I think of Roman, and then I blink, re-focusing, picturing Quinn seething back in the woods, furious that I left without an explanation. She will expect me to attack the lot of them and fail, but that's not my plan.

I approach without incident, joining a pair of girls who take turns chopping root vegetables with a hatchet. They don't look up right away. I quietly unfold the cloth satchel of seeds onto their work surface—an old wooden tray. The younger of the two, a girl with brown skin and limp arms, sits back on her heels. Her mouth falls open. Before I can place my hand over it to prevent a vocal reaction, she does it herself. Her knuckles are dry and cracked, a network of fine cobwebs.

"What are you doing?" she whispers, her eyes puffy.

"Just pretend I've always been here. Act normal."

She passes me water like she knows I'm dying of thirst. I gulp it down and wipe my chin.

"Keep it," she says. I tuck the bottle in my pants.

"Wren?" the other girl says. She brings down the hatchet and the end of a parsnip launches into the air. One of the boys lifts his head, but then swats at an insect.

"Add them to whatever you're making."

"I can't," she says, shaking her head. "They're toxic. One seed's enough to kill—"

"A grown man, I know. I read the Manual. You'll need at least eleven." I do a quick head count, cracking my neck in the process. "They kill girls too. Just don't get them on your hands."

She dumps the seeds into a pot, the other girl hurling root vegetables carelessly on top, water splashing. She has a massive bump on her forehead.

"How'd you get that?" I ask, the remaining seeds tumbling onto a patch of grass between us.

She shrugs and remains silent.

"Add more." I'm agitated and loud. It gets the attention of Rifle Boy.

"Hey!" he shouts. "Quit talking over there. We're hungry."

Clover and I make eye contact. It's the first time she realizes I'm back. Her expression is one of both alarm and hope. I start to rise from my crouched position, a few rogue canary peas spilling out at my feet. She subtly shakes her head *no*, but I can't help myself. I stand up straight, my fists clenched at my sides. Rifle Boy, who turned away after making the comment, now looks in my direction again. He separates himself from the group.

"Hey, I said we're hungry." He walks toward me. When he's within six feet of me, I see that he's older than the others. Hardened, with a scar on his neck and the biceps of a laborer. "What's with the eye patch?" He laughs, turns his back to me, and mumbles something about a pirate to the group of boys. When he turns back around, I sucker-punch him in his face—hard.

He stumbles back and holds his cheek, his nose. The boys scramble to their feet, but no one knows how to react. It's like they're waiting for instruction. I seize the moment of their indecision and disarm the boy I've just struck, kicking him in the stomach and sliding the rifle off his back.

When he recovers, I look him in the eyes. He can't focus. He just holds onto his cheek, testing his nose to see if it's broken. A stream of spit catches the wind and dangles from his chin like a fishing line.

"Make your own food," I tell him.

He wipes his face and yells at the boys, who stand like spectators at a show, "Go find Emmett. Tell him to prep the boat."

The boat? My heart canters.

A few of them take off downhill toward the beach. The others continue to pace awkwardly on the fringes of the cooking area. I toss the rifle to Clover, which I realize is stupid because she can't use one of her hands, but she catches it between her forearms.

"You're not going to find him," I tell him.

He spits. "And why's that?"

"Because he's dead."

"Yeah, right," he scoffs. "As if."

"As if what?"

"As if any of you could take on Emmett."

"Big guy? Curly hair? Vest with too many pockets?" He pauses.

"If you don't believe me, go look for him. You can tell him dinner is almost ready. Big man like that's gotta eat."

He steps in close so no one else can hear, and places a pair of ragged fingers on my collarbone. "I will. And don't skimp on the portion sizes. Watching you girls work is exhausting. I'm sure it'll be just as satisfying on the Mainland."

I want to spit in his face, but I don't, even though I'm subconsciously working the saliva through my teeth. Instead, I stare at his cheekbone, which is already swollen, and nod. "Want me to kiss it better?"

He laughs and backs away, wagging his tongue. "You're a feisty one, aren't you?" He looks at the remaining boys and nods toward the beach. "Go."

The boys start the descent. The blonde girl hangs back, mouth moving. I can't tell if she's even speaking. I go toward her, drawn in by her sunken eyes and filthy skin. Her marked-up arms. I want to know what her deal is, but as I open my mouth to speak, I'm yanked to the ground by my hair. From somewhere, a gasp.

Rifle Boy steps over me, showing off a fistful of my hair. My scalp burns; my eyes flutter. He releases the nest of strands into the wind and then grabs my shirt, twisting, lifting me a few inches off the ground, his face in mine. "You better learn to cooperate," he says in a half-whisper, half-grunt. "I don't want a back-talking servant. You ain't gonna save the Mainland—fix it all up for us—like that."

He lets go. I land with a thud, knocking my breath out of me. I turn my cheek just in time, as his spit hits my ear and pools inside. He nudges the blonde, who's been watching the whole time. She won't make eye contact. Beyond the Hill, the clouds are full, blackening. A chill ripples through the air.

When they're out of earshot, Clover rushes to my side. "You're going to get us killed."

"Thanks for the vote of confidence," I stutter, massaging my aching head. I stare at the open cut and take her elbow. There's a gash across the bottom of her hand, almost the length of her wrist, split open like a clamshell. I get a glimpse of flesh—yellow, the consistency of jelly—deep in the crevasse. I look away for a second and gag into the wind. "You need to clean that or it's going to get infected." I look for my water bottle, but I can't find it.

She draws her hand away. "Is he really dead?" she asks. "The big guy? Did you kill him?"

"He is."

"How'd you do it?"

"It doesn't matter." I tell one of the girls who'd been chopping the parsnips to take Clover into the woods. "Put some aloe on it and get it bandaged up." The girl nods and leads Clover away. I call for Quinn, cupping my hands around my mouth, yelling in the direction of the forest. I don't see her, and I try again. This time, she emerges with a prisoner, further up from where I left her. The other guard. He walks with his hands up. Quinn follows behind, her spear aimed at the space between his shoulder blades. The other girls stop what they're doing to watch.

"Hurry up," I holler. But she doesn't. She takes her time, indulging in the attention of the younger girls. When they get close, she stops. "Sit," she commands. He obeys and lowers himself to his knees like he's about to be executed. "Don't move."

I wave her several feet away, where he won't be able to hear our conversation. She drags her spear behind her, and it carves a line through a dusty portion of the path that goes down to the beach, as if to tell the boy: *do not cross.*

"What's happening?" she asks.

"They went to find Emmett."

"He's dead."

"Thanks for the reminder. I was there, remember?"

Quinn furls her brows, annoyed. "Then why would they go looking for him? Didn't you tell them?"

"They didn't believe me." I look around. "We probably only have a few minutes before they come back. We need to prioritize. Untie anyone who's bound and figure out a way to make sure these buffoons eat the canary peas when they get back." The wind picks up.

"Wait," Quinn says. "They went to the beach?"

"I told you. To look for Emmett." I bend to untie the gag in one of the Forager's mouths. She exhales in relief.

"What about Blue? Lennon?"

I swallow a gasp before it has a chance to become audible. I forgot about the girls on the beach.

"Wren? What about Blue and Lennon?"

"They're—they're fine," I stutter.

"Fine? Aren't they down there alone?"

Panic rises up inside me, the same hurricane of emotion I felt when I forgot the head count and Harlow went missing. I take a deep breath and attempt to exhale calmly, but the air comes out disjointed and uneven, like an engine failing to turn over.

"You forgot about them," Quinn says, "didn't you?"

"They're fine."

"You're not very convincing."

"They'll know what to do."

Quinn stares at me, scrutinizing my face. "You send a troop of them down there to find out their leader's been knocked off and you think Lennon and Blue will just know what to do?"

"Abbott's there."

"So? He's one of them."

"I think he's on our side." I recall the *X* behind his ear.

She folds her arms across her chest. "Just like Roman, right?" The prisoner shifts himself off his knees to his side. "I told you to sit!" Quinn yells.

The guard puts his hands up defensively and returns to his knees.

"You messed up," Quinn says. "You better hope you're right. You better hope they'll know what to do. Harlow might have been on both of us, but if we lose Lennon and Blue? That's all you."

CHAPTER 22

Section 6.7 – Severe weather warning signs
include: warm temperatures, darkening
skies, cumulous clouds, and high humidity.

QUINN STORMS TOWARD the cooking fire, leaving her
prisoner behind. He's tall, with a protruding forehead
and dark, recessed eyes. He slumps down onto his
elbow. He looks more tired than threatened. He stares
at me blankly.

"What?"

He yawns and says, "Nothing."

"Then keep your mouth shut."

He mockingly spreads his hand, which is large and
imposing, over his mouth. His knuckles are perfect. Not
a nick or scratch. Soft and lazy.

"What are you doing here?"

He removes his hand but doesn't speak.

"Answer the question."

"You told me to keep my mouth shut."

I squat and look him in the eyes. "Speak."

"You really don't know anything, do you?"

"Answer the question," I say again, my teeth clenched. "Why'd you come here?"

"We came for *you*," he whispers and then smiles, which turns into a laugh. It's a dark laugh, the same color as the changing sky. It's going to rain.

"We're not going anywhere."

"Oh, but you are," he replies calmly. "The Colony doesn't play very fair. Hoarding all the resources, stealing all of our women, taking our girls. They take ours; we take theirs. Which means"—he pauses for effect—"we take you."

Roman's words play in my brain. *The Mainland is getting low on girls*. The Colony's supposed to be a secret. "How did you find out?" I ask, abandoning the naive card.

"About the Hill?" he smirks.

"The Colony."

"Well, that there information isn't for me to share."

I kick his ribs. "Tell me."

He cowers, cradling his spleen. "You'll have to ask our fearless leader."

"Your leader's dead."

"Hex is dead?"

"Emmett. Dead as a washed-up sperm whale."

The guard smirks. "Emmett's no leader. He was just an old guy with a boat. You want answers about the Colony, Hex is your boy."

"No one's my boy."

"Well, if you decide you want answers, look for the one with the Storm Rider Multi-Shot." He mimics the sound of a gun.

202

Rifle Boy. I point to the weapon, now slung clumsily over a Forager's shoulders. "You mean that?"

He straightens. In the distance, Quinn examines a Collector with a black eye. "I gotta say, I didn't believe it at first."

"Believe what?"

"'Bout the Colony. 'Til my sister went missing. Then Hex done got lucky."

"How do you mean?"

"What's your name?"

"Wren." I immediately regret telling him my name.

"You know how to make a woman go mad, Wren?"

"You leave her on a Hill with a bunch of unwanted male thugs"—I look up—"in an impending storm?"

"Nah." He stares at me. "That ain't it. You take away her baby."

You take away her baby.

"Stay here."

The rain starts. I search for Quinn, trying to make sense of what he's said, wondering if he's already been into the canary peas. A Forager tries to protect the fire, but the wind is savage, blowing sideways, whipping flames and braids.

"Quinn," I holler, the sky collapsing from white to black in mere seconds, a lid on a pot. The rain switches to hail and pummels my shoulders. I shield my face and look back on the guard, stretched out on the grass, eyes skyward, succumbing to whatever nature might levy.

I hurdle over him and run uphill toward Quinn, the excavated ground sliding beneath me. I scream out her name. Girls scramble for shelter, everyone fleeing up, the way animals do.

"Quinn!" The rain beating down on my skull is the only noise I hear.

She emerges from the Quarters. "Come here!" She extends her hand, hesitates for a second, and then throws herself out of the shelter and skids down the hillside, her feet barely lifting off the ground. Ten feet away, she loses control.

I mutter, "Oh no," and brace for the impact, but she still manages to knock the wind out of me when we crash to the ground.

"Sorry."

I struggle to my feet, yanking my pants up, which are heavy with mud and barely clinging to my hips. "Get everyone in the Quarters. The Mothers and Smalls too. Clover. Get them all into the shelter."

"Where are you going?"

The rain falls sideways now. "I'm going to the beach to get Blue and Lennon."

"What about *him*?"

I glance at the guard. "Don't worry about him. He can take care of himself."

The guard doesn't move, accepting his fate. A death wish.

Quinn shrugs and surveys the hill. "Where are the Mothers and the Smalls?"

"The Hunter's Cabin. Go!" I grab her shoulders and spin her in the direction of the woods. "Go, Quinn! I'll meet you back in the shelter."

I turn to leave, but she follows me and grabs onto my hand.

"Wait!" Her eyes plead.

"There's no time to wait," I yell. "Anouk won't make it in this storm. It'll take her forever to recover."

She lets go of my hand. I don't look back, making a beeline for the beach instead. I feel ridiculous, slipping from one foot to the other like it's my first time on legs. Rain makes the Hill dangerous, especially after an excavation. I can barely see, but I strain to avoid anything that looks metal out of fear that I'll sever a limb.

I skid to a halt when I reach the path that winds down to the beach. From this position, I can only see a mere 10 percent of it. There are no boys. If they knew anything about survival, they'd know to go up. Higher ground.

I bypass the tunnel that Roman and Quinn used and pull out my knife. I can almost hear the swoosh of the blade slicing though the air as I move with purpose, my steps heavy and light at the same time.

The beach is deserted. One of the boats on the shore has been tipped upright and fills quickly with water. The fourth boat—the one that had been anchored in the water—is gone, carried out by the storm, a sacrifice. As if the sea hasn't taken enough already. I think back to the Colony books about the sea swallowing up entire cities.

A wave five times the size of the others pounces like an animal and knocks me backward. I climb to my feet and sidestep over to the cave. It's empty. No fishing gear, no boys, no girls. I hit the edge of the opening with my palm and begin to cry. I can't tell my tears from the sea spray or the rain.

The ocean continues its assault, lashing my ankles and the backs of my thighs, knocking me down. I feel like succumbing to the sea. Maybe it's me it's come for. Maybe I'm the sacrifice. Everything was in order until I became the Head Girl. Maybe I have to leave for things to return to the way they were.

For a second, I stand up with my back to the ocean and think about falling backward and going out with the next wave—but it also crosses my mind that I'm going mad.

"Wren!"

Am I hearing things? There's too much noise. I tuck my sopping hair behind my ears and look around. I drop my knife and immediately pounce to retrieve it before it disappears into a swirl of angry water.

"Wren!" Louder this time. "What are you doing?"

It's coming from above, from the sky gods. I throw my head back to listen, but I'm met with alarmed expressions instead.

Lennon and Blue lie belly-down on the cliff over the cave. They are so tightly positioned that, for a second, they look like a two-headed person.

"H-how d-did you g-get up th-there?" I stutter through chattering teeth. "Th-that's impossible to c-climb."

A rope begins to descend, dropping closer and closer in a jerking fashion. When it's almost in reach, it drops too low and slaps me in the face.

"Ouch." I cradle my cheekbone.

"Grab on."

A male voice. Abbott? I can't see. I wrap my calloused hands around the rope, which is monstrously thick, like the tail of a beast. Ember. My lost girl.

"Do you have it?" Blue's voice.

"Yes."

"Hold on."

I clinch my inner thighs against the rope, every muscle in my body contracted. The first part of the ascent is a smooth ride. I sway only slightly as I'm distanced from the sand, and then I slam into the cliff above the cave. My left shoulder drags against the rock for the remainder of the ascent. By the time I reach the top, I can't even speak. My mouth hangs open in a mute scream. I've left a trail of flesh up the side of the rock.

Lennon rips off the sleeve of her shirt and bundles it into a tight wad. She presses it into my shoulder, and I pass out.

CHAPTER 23

Section 6.9 – Debris and trash that washes up within the boundaries of the Hill's shoreline may be collected and repurposed.

WHEN I COME to, I feel like I've been asleep for days. The sun beats, but my clothes are still damp. Lennon sings softly beside me. A lullaby. The same one my Mother used to sing before she Departed. When Lennon finishes, I ask her to sing it again.

The second time she reaches the chorus, I sit up, surveying my surroundings for the first time. Panic sets in. "Where is everyone?"

"Safe up in the Quarters."

"Everyone?"

"Everyone but us," she says. "Not that we're not safe—we're just not up there."

"Where's Blue?"

"She's in the Quarters too."

"But . . . how did you escape? The boys. They came down here searching for Emmett. How did you get away?"

"The one who looks like you? He helped."

"I told Quinn he was on our side."

"He tied us up, but it was a hoax. Thief knot. Then he volunteered to stand guard. At first the boys weren't buying it, but then the storm came, and they took off. You should have seen them, Wren. Chaos. Like they'd never seen rain before."

"Took off where?"

"I don't know. I assumed they would have gone up to the shelter. The cliffs, maybe? They were looking for a boat, supposedly anchored offshore."

I stare out at the open water. Nothing for miles, other than the oil rig. "Where's Abbott now?"

"The Quarters. With Blue."

"Why is he up there?" I scramble to my feet too quickly and get a head rush. Tiny stars flicker in front of my eyes. My shoulder throbs from where it dragged against the rock.

"One of the Smalls is sick. He said he might be able to help."

A feeling of sorrow settles in the back of my throat. "Anouk?"

Lennon nods.

"That's all he said?"

"Also that he's your brother."

"My what?"

"Your brother."

"What does he mean by that?"

She shrugs her shoulders. "No idea. He tried to explain, but his face turned red, and he kept tripping on his words. I think it has something to do with why you two look so much alike."

I don't know what to do with that information. I found a button once that said BIG BROTHERS ROCK over a picture of a guitar. I'd removed the pin part of it, turned into a fishing lure, and tossed the rest. Caught the largest dogfish anyone had ever seen. A few days later, I dug up a guitar, though unlike the picture on the button, it only had four strings. Whatever big brothers were, they had something to do with music.

"Are you okay to head up to the Quarters?" Lennon stands and slings her bag over her shoulders.

"How long have I been out?"

"Since yesterday." She sticks her finger in her mouth. "I have a loose tooth. Are you coming?"

"I need a minute."

She crosses her legs to sit back down.

"No." I make a *stop* gesture with my hand. "You go ahead. I'll be up shortly."

She looks unsure about leaving me, but quietly agrees. "You know what else he said?" She pulls her socks, which are odd and spotted, up over her knees.

"What?"

"He said you had the same Mother."

"The same *Mother?*"

"Right? Ridiculous. Blue and I laughed in his face."

I muster a smile, but inside, my head is in turmoil. Why would he say that? What's next? "Tell Quinn I'll be up in a minute."

She turns, the weapon she fashioned jutting out of her pack. She rushes uphill for about twenty paces when her body gives way to fatigue, and she drags herself the rest of the way.

I remain seated at the top of the cliff. I stretch my legs, sit tall, and take a much-needed breath. The sun warms my shoulders like a shawl, but I still shiver. I think of Dasha, my assigned Mother. Her hair was down to her waist, but it was always braided in some intricate knot. When she took it out at the end of the day, her hair would be bent and curled in opposite directions, like wires from broken electronics. I found so much comfort in that blanket of hair. I used to fall asleep twirling it around my fingers. I couldn't imagine a Mother with short hair.

I think of Abbott's claim that we shared her. It's so far-fetched, so impossible, that I know I'm missing something. I consider the possibility that Dasha became his Mother as her assignment when she went to the Mainland.

The beach below me is covered in post-storm debris. Seaweed, shells, driftwood, pinecones, leaves, even a buoy litter the shoreline like toys that haven't been put away. I head down to see if there's anything useful, not ready to part with my solitude. The calm before the next storm, which will be man-made. I know they'll be back.

I throw the rocks into the ocean and kick the seaweed into a pile in the middle of the beach. The buoy is hazard-orange with a black tip. Six feet of rope, frayed and mint green are attached to it. I pull it along behind me and examine the rest of the beach.

A shoe rolls on top of the surf like it's being vomited up. I step forward and let it wash into me. It's mostly white, with a thick lace that's still knotted, albeit loose. It's big. It won't fit anyone on the Hill, but the lace will be useful. I throw the buoy behind me and start picking at the knot when the matching shoe comes into sight, still attached to the body floating toward me, facedown.

CHAPTER 24

Section 6.5 – Switchgrass, soybeans, algae, wheat, and corn are all suitable biofuel crops.

I DRAG HIM to shore by his ankles, which feels undignified. But he's heavy, and my shoulder can barely take the load. His head leaves a shallow tunnel in the sand as I pull him clear of the water. Despite his bluish lips and disheveled hair, he is recognizable. The guard with the missing sister. Quinn's prisoner.

I fold his hands so they rest on his stomach, not far from where I kicked his rib cage earlier, and not out to the sides, which gives the impression that he's given up. He looks more peaceful this way. The second dead body in two days. It's as if the Hill itself is fighting back for us. I crumple to the ground and lie beside him, unsure of what else to do. The sun blinds me, and then the light is blocked out entirely.

Roman stands in its place. He offers his hand. "Get up," he says. "They're coming back."

I stagger to my feet on my own. More stars, like a flashback to midnight, glow in my periphery. He stares at my mangled shoulder, repulsed. "They found his body," he says, "in the tunnel."

"How'd they know he was there?"

"I'm guessing it was the backpack resting just outside it."

I avoid eye contact.

"They think you killed him."

"But he fell."

We both look at the body in the sand.

"And he drowned. I swear I just pulled him out of the water."

"They're stuck," he says. "They don't know how to get back to the Mainland without Emmett. They're stuck, and they're angry."

"They can go back the same way they came."

"Do you even know how they got here?"

I don't say anything because it's an ongoing theme these days. I don't know.

"Emmett's boat is how they got here. Emmett's boat, which is probably halfway to the equator by now, thanks to that tropical storm."

"How do you know all this?"

"You said it yourself. I know this place better than anyone." He looks down at the body between us. "We need to move him."

"Where?"

"Off the beach. They don't need any more reason to want to kill you."

"They want to kill me?"

"They do now." Roman squats beside the body and places his arm under the boy's back. He lets out an exaggerated exhale like he's in pain, as he lifts him over his shoulder and returns to a standing position.

Paranoid, I look around but don't see anyone. "We have a small graveyard in the Westside Forest. We can bury him up there."

"The Westside Forest? You think I'm carrying him all the way up there?"

"I'll help you."

"What, are you going to say a few words too? Have a wake?"

"What's a wake?"

"Never mind," he snaps. His voice makes me flinch. He kicks the ground, causing the limbs of the body he's carrying to swing recklessly. Then he stops. "Sorry," he mutters, pressing on toward the path that leads uphill. "I didn't mean to yell. It's just—we don't have time to dig a grave and give this guy a funeral. This isn't over, Wren. Not even close. They're determined to get back to the Mainland, and they're hell-bent on you coming with them—if they don't kill you before then."

"One of them claims he's my brother."

"Your brother?" Roman heads off the path toward the tunnel opening Quinn revealed earlier. He stumbles and falls on top of the body as he lays him in a shallow depression past the tunnel. "Your brother. That's just about the most ridiculous thing I've heard."

"What does he mean by it?"

Roman runs his hands down his face like he wants to pull his skin off in frustration.

"I'm sorry," I say, throwing my hands up. "I don't know what it means."

"I know," he says. "And I'm really trying to help you."

"But what?"

"But nothing. I didn't say anything." He scoops up piles of leaves and needles and covers the body. "Which one?"

"His name's Abbott."

"The one who was guarding the beach?"

"He looks like me."

"If he *is* your brother, and I don't know how that's possible, then it means you share the same—"

I cut him off. "Mother, I know. Like I said—crazy."

"Or father," he says.

"Right." I nod. "Or father." I don't know what a father is, but I don't dare admit it. I practice my unsurprised face and gather my hair into a messy ponytail at the top of my head. As I struggle to collect the loose pieces and jam them into the worn elastic, I'm aware that he's watching me.

"What?"

"Nothing," he says, in a way that implies I've caught him off guard.

I study his face. His cheeks are still flushed from carrying the body uphill, and his hair sticks up with a mix of sea salt and sweat. He looks shipwrecked and beautiful. My heart starts to gallop like it's been stung by a bee, and for a second, I forget about fathers and mothers and dead bodies.

Then I kiss him. Not on the cheek like I kiss the girls, but on the mouth. He wraps his hands around the back of my head and kisses me back. It's kind of hard, like we're being pushed together by an angry mob, his tongue lashing the inside of my mouth. A swirl of heat rushes through my lower half. Then he pulls back.

I take a breath and attempt to steady myself. I feel like a doll, limbs heavy, body loose. And then he pulls me back in and kisses me again. Lighter this time, diffusing my adrenaline.

Suddenly, a rock whizzes past a tree and bounces off the ground beside us. It lands on the buried body, making us both cringe. Neither of us thinks to duck. Quinn would already be on the ground by now. I bat the air like it's in the way.

"Roman!"

We both look uphill. Finn steps out from behind a tree. Roman rolls his eyes and waves him down. Quinn follows behind him. Roman and I exchange puzzled glances as the pair approaches.

"Nice," Quinn says. Her gaze cuts me, and I have to look away. "We're all up there thinking you're in danger and cleaning up Anouk's vomit, and you're down here having a little mouth party."

"A mouth party?" Roman says.

Finn spits. His eye has only deflated slightly from the other day.

"We were down here burying a body."

"A body?" Quinn asks. "And where did you bury it? In his mouth?"

I bend down and swat away a heap of leaves, revealing an ear. She shivers and shuts her mouth. Finn squints, as though he might actually be able to identify him by his ear. "Who is it?"

"Quinn should recognize him. He was her prisoner."

She bends down and picks the leaves off his face, one at a time. "How did you kill him?"

"I didn't kill him. I pulled him out of the water like this. He drowned."

Roman turns toward Finn. "What are you doing here?"

"You framed two sides of a house and then took off. Your dumb dog tried to follow."

Ember.

"Draco," Roman says, distant. "It was an emergency."

"Who, her?" Finn nods at me, disgusted.

"I'm not an emergency."

"Don't take offense," Finn replies. "My brother's always trying to play rescue hero."

Brother. That word. Roman reaches out and pushes Finn in the head.

Finn brings his elbows up in defense. "You want an emergency, try roofing a house with only two walls. In a bloody storm."

I cut in, "No one was rescued."

"No kidding." Finn ducks under Roman's imposing hand and spits again. "You better get home soon.

Colony's not gonna be happy if they find out you're messing around on the Hill, let alone making out with one of its inhabitants."

"And you think they're going to be happy when they find out the Hill's been attacked and their girls taken to the Mainland?"

"No one's taking us to the Mainland," I say. "Emmett's dead; this guy too." I nudge the leafy body with my foot. "Abbott's up in the Cabin, and Quinn already took out the other guard."

"What's your plan, Wren?" Roman asks, frustrated.

"I have a few."

"Is kissing them goodbye one of them?" Quinn snaps.

I glare at her and face him. "We had canary peas. Don't know what's left of them after the storm. And we have a weapon. Plus two of them are girls. Untrained. Easy to pick off."

"See, dear brother? Looks like no one here needs saving today."

Roman steps toward Finn.

"Save it," Finn says. "We have arrangements. You know that. Don't screw it up because of her."

Arrangements?

Roman looks down toward the beach. "Someone needs to keep watch."

"We don't need advi—" Quinn says.

I interrupt, "What does he mean by arrangements, Roman?"

Quinn and I exchange glances and wait for his reply. He doesn't.

"You know what, never mind," I say impatiently. "We'll be okay. We'll figure it out."

"They're going to attack."

"And we'll be ready this time."

He puts his hands on my shoulders. "Listen to me," he says, which seems unnecessary, given that he's shouting in my face. "You know the tunnel where I found you? The one where you came tumbling out of the entrance, and I gave you my flashlight?"

"I don't know if I *tumbled.*"

"Slipped, fell, whatever. There's another way out of there."

"Other than that?" I point behind him toward the existing exit.

"There's another. A tunnel within a tunnel. It runs deeper underground. I don't think they've discovered it."

I don't remember seeing another way out of that tunnel. "Where?"

"Against the rear wall. Put your back to the light of the exit. It looks like a pile of rocks from a cave-in, but they're stable. Climb up. The entrance to the tunnel is on the other side."

"Where does it lead?" Quinn sounds unenthused.

"It leads to our village," he says. "It's a long way, but there are rooms off to the sides if you need to stop."

"Great," Finn says. "Now they know where we live."

"Does that threaten you?" I ask.

"Threaten me? You?" He laughs. "No. Well, maybe her." He gestures toward Quinn, who bows in response.

"What, are you best friends now?" I get in his face. "What's the problem?"

Finn places a heavy hand on my shoulder. I wince in pain. "Since my brother failed to explain the little arrangement we have, let me explain," he says. "We lease our land, aka the Great Bear Landfill, aka the Hill, to the Colony, for whatever crazy reason the Colony has for you all living here like a pack of ferals. Social experiment? Training ritual? Don't know, don't care, you decide. In exchange, they give us stuff. It's quite the operation they run over there. Food production, technology, medicine. Most importantly, they have a healthy supply of methanol." He lays a fist on my other shoulder. "And then there's our friends on the Mainland. Beyond disease and the odd black-market score, they don't have much to offer, but they can't live without our custom-made biodiesel. Choppers don't fly on will and propellers alone."

"We can't make the biodiesel without the Colony's methanol," Roman sighs.

"So, yes," Finn continues. "Stay on your Hill and keep doing your little digs or whatever it is you do here. We like things just the way they are—or were, before you got inside my brother's mouth."

I go to hit him hard with an uppercut to the chin, but Roman intervenes by grabbing my wrist. I twist myself free. "Just go," I tell him. "We have things to do."

He looks at me apologetically, but on behalf of whom, I don't know. Finn turns uphill. Roman opens his mouth to speak, but I turn my back and grab Quinn's arm. I deviate from the path, making a direct line for the Rock. She half-runs to keep up with my pace. It's Quinn who looks back at Finn and Roman. I don't know what she sees.

CHAPTER 25

Section 6.3 – Signs of infection include
fever, red skin around the injury, pus,
swelling, blisters, and pain.

WHEN WE REACH the Rock, I whistle three times to initiate a head count. The shrillness gives me a headache. We wait in silence for the girls to emerge. Quinn's eyes and slumped posture speak of despair.

"You kissed him," she says.

"That was meant to be private."

"But it wasn't."

I stare at her, unsure what she wants me to say, unsure of how to make it hurt less. *Sorry?*

"What was it like?"

"I don't know." I shudder with embarrassment. "Kind of wet. Same as kissing a girl." *And lovely*, I add in my head. I don't describe how it made my whole body come alive. How even thinking about it now causes my muscles to tighten.

"Was it planned?"

"No. It just happened." I brush my hair out of my face. "Did it look planned?"

She shakes her head. "It looked kind of special. A little bit rough—passionate."

"Maybe."

"And sort of disgusting."

"A little bit."

"I wish it was me."

We lock eyes. I don't know if she means she wishes she were kissing him—or me.

A line of girls appears uphill near the Quarters, and I feel like my chest might explode with anticipation.

"Here they come."

"Yep," Quinn sighs. "Here they come."

I pace in front of the Rock as the girls descend, scanning the group for Arrow, but she's hidden behind a mass of legs. I only get a glimpse of her red hair. I resist breaking through the crowd to get her. Instead, Clover manipulates her way through the tangle of girls and reaches me first. She's almost unrecognizable—her eyes are weary and recessed, and a sweep of dried blood marks her forehead like paint. She lifts a trembling finger to my face.

"This is all your fault," she slurs.

I grab her accusing finger and fold it back into her hand. It's her injured wrist I'm interested in. Sounds like infection is talking.

"Let me see it." When she recoils and pulls her bandaged arm away, I repeat, "Let me see it."

I take hold of her elbow and she yelps. I unravel the

fabric, which is damp with blood in some areas, hard and crusted in others. When I reach the wound, the smell is so foul, I stumble backward.

"You're sick, Clover. You need help."

Her eyes flutter, and she leans on me with her full body weight. She is eerily warm.

"Quinn, go after them."

"Who?"

"Finn and Roman. Clover needs help."

"We did a couple rounds of aloe."

"Have you seen this?" I raise Clover's wrist in the air. "We're talking an amputation here. No plant will fix this."

"Are there any pills left in the Quarters?"

I shake my head. "We used them all on Nova after the whole nail-in-her foot incident. Go." I point to another girl, a mighty one, only ten but with legs that could out-run us all. "You go with her."

Quinn and the fast girl take off and I cautiously lower Clover to the ground, so she's lying on her back. I use the sleeve of my shirt and her sweat to wipe the blood off her forehead. "Someone get me some water."

Lennon steps in with a canteen and touches it to Clover's lips. It's an awkward size and shape, and she pours water all over Clover's face. I catch what drips down her neck and attempt to hand-feed her.

"I don't need water," Clover mumbles. She makes a feeble attempt to push our meddling hands away.

When I'm confident some has made it down her throat, I take the canteen from Lennon and set it aside.

"There's a village on the north side of the island. They have some equipment there—more than we have. And medicine. They can help you."

"No," she cries, face anguished. "I'm not going anywhere. *'Outside of the Hill's boundary, girls cannot survive.'* Section 2.2."

"You won't survive if you stay. Section 6.3: INFECTION MANAGEMENT."

She stares up at me.

"You don't have a lot of time, Clover. They'll take care of you."

"*'Girls over the age of ten caught attempting to leave the Hill'*—she slurs—*'will be stripped of their identity, banished from the Colony, and . . .'*"

I place a hand over her mouth. "You won't."

One of the Smalls starts crying, and then others join in, as if by invitation. I want to yell at them to shut up, but I remind myself they're traumatized. I put my finger to my lips and gently shush them. "Head count." No one stands in the correct order. Girls pace. Girls cry. A couple just sit. One rocks back and forth; another is motionless, her knees bent and wrapped tight into her chest. Still, no one cooperates. "Head count," I yell.

"One, two, three . . ."

The numbers come from all directions but stop at seven.

"Eight," I yell. "Number eight, count yourself." Silence. "Mothers, if eight is one of your charges, count her in." I glance downhill. Four figures are making their way up. I feel a rush of relief. Quinn has managed to track down Finn and Roman. I squat, whisper into Clover's ear that she's going to be okay, and then I stand back up. "Number eight," I shout again, turning in a slow circle so everyone can hear me. "Number eight, count yourself."

Then everything around me stops, like a bird flying against the wind. Mouths continue to move, but I can't hear any sounds. It's as though they've all been turned off.

On the outskirts of the crowd is Abbott—the boy who looks like me, my supposed brother, fever-pale and looking profoundly sad. In his arms is the tiny, lifeless body of Anouk. Number eight.

CHAPTER 26

Section 2.2 – Outside of the Hill's boundary, girls cannot survive.

MY HANDS TREMBLE and my legs give way. It doesn't matter that we all knew it was going to happen, with the way it took her so long to hold her head up, to sit on her own, to walk. She was a mistake. The Colony should never have sent her, and yet there was something about her vulnerability we all identified with. The fear, the uncertainty. She is like all of us.

Was.

I reach for the canteen and spill water over my face and down my throat, but I take in too much and choke. Girls back away like I'm contagious. Abbott waits quietly with the body still draped in his arms, one hand cradling her head. I will myself to stand, and Abbott passes her to me. She's wrapped loosely in a red blanket that looks like stemless flowers stitched together. It gives her the illusion of having pink cheeks. Of life.

She does not look peaceful or free. She looks and feels exhausted. Death tugs at her wrists and ankles. Even her fingers, usually dainty and soft like caterpillars, are heavy as lead. I do my best to tuck her feet and hands into the blanket and kiss her forehead. "I'm sorry," I whisper.

When I turn around, I notice the boys. Roman bends over Clover, examining her wrist. Finn is stoic. I stare at him with a pleading eye.

"Lennon," I say gently, as if Anouk is sleeping, and I'll wake her if I'm too loud.

Lennon separates herself from the others. She cries soundlessly, like she is still switched off, but her whole face is wet with tears. "Take her up to the Quarters. I'll be up as soon as Clover's gone."

Lennon pries Anouk from my arms. She adjusts the girl into a different position, tucks the blanket under her chin, propping up her head. Now she looks asleep. I turn away before that changes.

Finn looks around. "Do you have a stretcher?"

There's nothing but the Rock. I don't know what a stretcher is. Roman guesses this and clarifies what his brother is looking for. "Something to carry her on. It's a long walk."

"I can walk," Clover insists.

"You can't even stand." I look for a Collector. "Anyone have any ideas?'

A blonde girl missing a tooth says, "We can rig a hammock?"

"Do you have a shovel?" Roman looks at the group

of the girls. "It's a broad blade attached to a handle. You use it to dig."

"Look around this place," I say sarcastically. "We pretty much invented the shovel."

Roman throws his hands up in an *I can't win* gesture.

"Come." I wave for him to follow me to the Quarters. We're not far behind Lennon, who moves uphill at a good pace. Part of Anouk's red blanket has unraveled, and it waves in the wind like a somber flag.

"She was sick from day one." Emotion rushes my face and tingles my nose.

"It happens," he says. "My brother died when he was only a week old. We tried to get him to the Mainland, but he never made it."

"I'm sorry." We walk in silence. "To the Colony? Is that where you were trying to take him?"

"A hospital. Not everyone on the Mainland is bad, Wren. There's good people there, too, trying to rebuild. What my brother had . . . it was far too complicated to treat. He was only this big." Roman approximates the size with his hands. A length similar to my forearm.

"I've never seen a baby that small," I say. "When our babies arrive, they're kind of big and sturdy. Some already have their teeth. Occasionally, they can already sit up on their own." Or talk, I think, in my own case.

"Then you've never seen an infant," he says. "They're small in a way you can't imagine. And they're completely helpless. You look at them and wonder how they can possibly have all the working parts to make it to adulthood." Roman pauses. We are midway to the Quarters. "I guess my brother never did."

I want to ask him about Finn and his Mother, but Roman's quiet for the remainder of the ascent.

Leaning against the outer wall of the Quarters is the Collector's gear: shovels, picks, axes, rakes. The tools on the end are slated for repair. I take a broken rake and a broom with a detachable head and hand them to Roman.

"Will these work?"

He attempts to bend the broom handle, gripping each end and pressing down against his raised knee. He nods.

"Wait here." Inside the sleeping area, I dismantle Quinn's hammock. Anouk is tucked into a tiny bed that one of the girls fashioned from old couch cushions. Lennon has brushed her hair out of her face. A little stuffed rabbit wearing a quilted vest is nestled beside Anouk's cheek. Though the toy's fur is singed and dirty and the ears threadbare, the eyes are intact and warm and loving. I rub the tingle from my nose, trying to keep the tears in. Lennon sits on her own bed and washes her blotchy face in a bowl of water.

Outside the entrance, I spread the hammock on the ground. "Pass me the broom." I thread the handle through a series of metal grommets along the top of the fabric. The other end of the hammock is plain, but Quinn had stitched canvas loops into the corners. Together we secure the rake so that both ends can be carried.

"This will work," he says, testing the fabric by pushing down with the heel of his hand. He starts downhill. "It may take a few days before she's strong enough to return. I'll bring her back."

"Thanks, Roman."

Before we close in on the girls, he stops, takes the stretcher off his shoulders, and brings it to his waist. "Come if you're in trouble, Wren. Use the tunnel."

I bring my end of the stretcher down and nod. The scene at the Rock is bewildered chaos. Some girls sit lifelessly; others pace erratically, as though they've been shipwrecked here. It's more how I pictured the arrival of the Departed Girls on the Mainland—or the Mainland itself.

We set the stretcher down beside Clover.

"Is that my hammock?" Quinn asks.

"Clover doesn't have one."

Quinn bites her lip. Together we lift Clover onto the stretcher. "They'll take care of you," I promise. "We'll see you in a few days."

"We have to head back," Finn says, thwarting any further delay.

I mouth *thank you*. He half-nods, his body language softening.

I place my hand over Clover's and give it a squeeze as the boys lift her off the ground. I rise with her, and she closes her eyes, as if she finally has permission to just be as sick as she is. I blow a kiss as the trio descends a few paces to clear the Rock and then turns north toward their village.

CHAPTER 27

Section 8.6 – Never trust a boy.

WHEN LENNON RETURNS from the Quarters, I restart the head count. There are twenty-seven of us—twenty-eight if you include Abbott. What the hell am I supposed to do with him? I'm certain that if he didn't look like me, I would have killed him by now, but he's quiet and cooperative and flying under the radar. And he's my brother." I make eye contact with him, and we stare at each other without interruption. It only breaks when Quinn shakes my arm.

"Do something," she says. "They need a leader."

She's right. Everyone looks lost and scared. I need to give a speech, but I don't know what to say because I, too, feel disoriented and drained. How much do I tell? How much do I hold back?

I go to the rear of the Rock, where it's easier to climb. I'll speak from up there. The height will give the illusion of power and confidence. I reach up, find a ledge with my fingertips, and then bring one foot up into an indent. I count to three and hoist myself up. My shoulder throbs, still raw from being dragged up the side of the cliff, but I make progress. By the time I reach the top, I already have their attention.

The words come out of me without thought, as though the speech was formed long ago and was simply waiting for the right circumstances to be delivered. "This is home. No black eye, no boy, no death, nothing can change that. You are still alive, and tonight you are safe."

A thin blanket of calm settles over them. Just enough to take off the chill.

"On the Mainland, we were a myth, the Colony a rumor." I stop for a minute to regain my footing, my heart a drum. "But now they know."

A Collector in a ratty jumpsuit asks, "Why do they want to take us to the Mainland?"

"Because we can do stuff. The Hill . . ." I wave my arm. "This used to be a garbage dump, but we've turned it into a home. We've made it work. We live off it. The Colony's trained us. Everything in the Manual has helped us survive."

A Hunter stands. "So what?"

"So think of the Mainland as a giant garbage dump. Imagine what we could do there."

"Great," she says. "The future I've always dreamed of. I thought we were supposed to go to the Colony?"

"We are, but it's not safe—at least not right now."

A Forager crosses her arms. "But it's okay to

send Clover off half-dead in a hammock with two boys?"

"They're not the enemy." I stand firm.

A girl points to her eye, swollen to the size of a piece of fruit. "No?"

Quinn jumps in. "Not—not all boys are bad," she stutters, unsure if she believes her own statement. "Some are, some aren't. It's complicated."

My heart balloons with gratitude. She's backing me up.

"And how are we supposed to know the difference?" asks a Collector.

Blue smirks. "A good question."

"The boys Clover left with live here on the island. There's a village up north."

"Where up north?"

"You know the black part of the map—"

"The head?"

"Yes. Up there."

"So you're telling us *those* boys are good," a girl starts.

"And the ones that attacked us from the Mainland are bad," another finishes.

"Yes." I nod. "Kind of."

A Hunter turns around. "Then what about *him*?" She points to Abbott. Everyone stares. A few girls stand. A Small, asleep on the ground, jerks in her sleep.

"He's . . ." I start. "He's . . ."

"I'm from the Colony," Abbott spits.

A Hunter raises her spear and fixes it on him. "Show

me the part in the Manual that says there's boys in the Colony."

My heart races. Quinn and I exchange nervous glances. I motion for Abbott to shut up.

"He's a boy servant," Quinn shouts.

The Hunter slowly lowers her spear. "Is that true?"

Abbott raises his hands. "It is. I'm a Colony servant."

Lennon, contemplative during the entire exchange, raises her hand. "So now what?"

"Anouk's Grounding Ceremony."

"And then?"

"Roman said the boys who attacked would be back."

"And Roman is . . . a good guy?" asks the Forager with the swollen eye.

"Wren's boy love," Quinn spurts.

My face steams. The girls look at me, perplexed and intrigued. Arrow stops rolling on the grass and looks up at me. "What does *boy love* mean?"

"It means nothing."

Quinn puckers her lips.

"They're coming back," I repeat, ignoring her. "They're trying to figure out a plan, but they were sent here to take us to the Mainland, and that's what they'll try to do."

"What about the Colony?" Blue asks. "How come they haven't sent any help?"

"The Colony needs *your* help," Abbott says.

Lennon squeezes her head between her hands. "This is all too much," she says, exasperated. "Can't we just bury her already?" She gestures uphill toward the Quarters, where Anouk is.

"Yes," I agree. "We shouldn't keep her waiting."

Abbott raises his eyebrows.

I climb down the side of the rock, sending the girls to the Quarters but holding the leaders back. There are five, representing the Hunters, Collectors, Suppliers, Foragers, and Mothers. The girls making their way to the shelter have thinned out from a mass to a staggered line, the Smalls mainly at the back, struggling to keep pace with the others.

"Anouk's Grounding Ceremony," I say. "You know the drill."

"Yes," Abena says, her voice mournful and far away.

"Quinn, you find and prepare the burial plot. Then come get the others for the ceremony."

Quinn nods. Abena raises her hand to speak. She is young, only a few days on the job. Her usually well-kept hair is ragged, like the ends have been chewed off by one of the babies, but her face is warm. The kind of face that could put you to sleep and give you good dreams. I feel guilty for letting her down. For not assigning more Mothers.

"Bring something to be buried with her," I say. "Something Anouk loved. Something she can take with her to the afterlife."

Abena nods solemnly.

"I'm sorry," I say. "We all knew it was coming. We all knew she wouldn't make it. I know there aren't enough Mothers. You're doing an amazing job."

"I couldn't do it," Quinn says.

Abena exhales, appreciative.

"After the Grounding Ceremony, free time. Let's let loose. The girls need it. We eat, we sing, we play. Anything you can think of to make it festive. I don't want anyone going to bed tonight afraid. Fear is what we need to conserve." I look up at the Rock. "We need to save as much fear as possible."

"For what?" the Supplier asks.

"For when they come back."

CHAPTER 28

Section 4.5 – Each Arrival shall be assigned
a Mother.

THE ASSIGNMENT LEADERS turn almost in unison and
head up toward the Quarters.

"Quinn," I shout, tugging at her shirt. "Wait."

She stumbles backwards. "What?" Her expression is
drained.

"Thank you," I say. "For having my back." I reach for
her hand, but she pulls away. She won't look at me. "I'm
sorry. I didn't know you were there. I would never have
kissed him like that if I had known."

"Do you love him?"

"*Love* him? Quinn, I just met him."

"But could you? Could you love him?"

"I don't know. I mean . . . I suppose."

Quinn drops her arms heavily. Her eyes fill. "I want
you to love me."

"I do love you."

"But—"

"Quinn, I couldn't even tell you if it was day or night right now, even though the sun is shining in my face." I squint and block a sunbeam with my hand. "I don't remember the last time I ate. I don't really understand what's happening on the Mainland, there's a dead Small up there. Clover might be next, and some Hex lunatic is planning another attack in a tunnel system we only found out existed yesterday."

I take a breath. "So I do *love* him? No. But did I like kissing him? Yes. I did. A lot. I can't help that. And if that sounds confusing, you might be right, Quinn, because I am confused."

She reaches for my hand. "But that doesn't have to change us. We'll always be us." Our fingers intertwine, and we lock eyes. The air hums between us. A minute goes by, then another. A pair of birds swoop overhead, rising and falling. She pulls me into her so our lips almost touch. Pause.

I close my eyes, and then her mouth is on mine, delicate but firm. Friendly, fierce. My breath catches. Slowly, Quinn pulls away and takes a step back. She turns and starts uphill.

When she is out of range, I burst into tears and stumble toward the Rock. I find my usual finger and footholds when Abbott shatters the silence.

"Need a hand?"

"Abbott, you scared me," I say, wiping my face.

"You okay?"

I nod and try to ground my shaking legs. So much for trying to conserve fear. I'm a live wire.

"Sorry."

"And no, I don't need a hand. Been scaling this thing since I was seven."

I get up to a portion of the Rock that is flat relative to the rest and stop to knock my hair out of my face. It throws my balance and I slip, one leg going straight down like a spike destined for the ground.

He acts quickly. Stepping in, he stops my foot with cupped hands before I'm in a full split.

I close my eyes with shame.

"You're welcome," he says. Without warning, he gives me a forceful boost, and I fly upward. I land on the top of the rock on all fours and face the ocean. The water barely moves. It shines flat in the sun like it's half-asleep. Far offshore, I think I see a boat, but it turns into a bird, then a buoy, then a seal, and then nothing. I need binoculars—or a second eye. I scoop up my shirt and jump off the Rock from its lowest point. When I hit the ground out of breath, Abbott stares at me with the kind of look that suggests he's about to tell me something I don't know.

"What?" I say, exhausted.

"Ever wonder why you have that patch on your eye?"

I cradle the patch affectionately.

"It was to stop you from getting sent to the Hill. An imperfection."

"My eye's partially blind."

"That's what Mom wanted everyone to believe. If you're blind now, it's from wearing it all the time, but you never were. Not when you were born," he says. "Your vision was perfect. Like mine."

My hand immediately darts to my face. He's lying. My eye flickers behind the patch in agreement. "So then what? It just became a decoration?"

"When the Colony figured out there was nothing wrong with you, they sent you to the Hill. You were almost five."

"Stop."

"I remember them putting you in the boat."

"You know nothing about me or my eye or my Mother."

"You screamed. I can still hear it. In my head, you've been screaming for nearly a decade." Abbott plugs his ears with his hands, fingers splayed.

"I said *stop*." I step into his space.

"Mom insisted you keep wearing the patch so that one day you could be identified. So that one day you could be found."

Always wear your patch.

"I didn't *want* to be found," I spit, unintentionally showering his cheek. "I just want everything to go back to normal."

Abbott wipes his face. "There's no more normal, Wren. Not since the Colony's been found out."

My shoulders slump wearily. "But how are you my brother?"

"Same mom, but I'm a year older than you."

"And taller," I say, looking up. "I suppose you're going to tell me that you're also my father."

"Sick—no!" Abbott says, defensive and confused. "Does the Manual not teach you this stuff?"

"The Manual teaches us that men are the enemy. Probably wouldn't be as convincing if we knew they also could be family."

"Mom—"

I interrupt. "My Mother left years ago. In a Departure Ceremony."

"No, Wren," he says. "The girl who got on that boat years ago was your Hill Mother." He pulls out a picture from deep inside a chest pocket. The photo is the size of his palm and is in pristine condition, unlike the scraps of photographs we find on the Hill, with scarcely a tenth of the image even remotely visible. "This is your real mother."

I study the image. This woman is fair-haired, sad-eyed, young. She looks my age, maybe slightly older, except she has a baby tucked under each arm, one swaddled in gauze-like cloth, the other bare-chested, clinging to her neck. The swaddled baby is tinier than our Smalls. I think of Roman's infant baby brother.

"This is me"—Abbott points to the larger baby on our mother's left—"and this is you."

I analyze the rest of the picture. The room is yellow. The edge of a metal table sits in the foreground. To the right, a window is open to a gray sky.

"I look blind."

"You were only a few hours old."

I study the picture for another minute, re-drawing it in my brain. Table, bed, babies, mom, window, sky. Then

I shove it back at him, as though it might combust and burn my fingers. Abbott places it inside a zipped pocket and pulls out another. "Now what?"

"This is the last photo taken of you."

I snatch it from him. The picture is facedown. I wish I kept it that way.

I am older than in the first image, screaming. My mother screams too. Our arms reach for each other, but we are separated. Someone holds my mother back. There are arms around her waist, wrapped on top of the other, a coiled snake. I'm in someone else's arms, about to be placed in a boat. My eye is patched. Instinctively, I reach up and touch the fabric ribbing.

I flip the picture over and shove it back at him. I don't want to memorize it, though my mother's anguished face is already stamped in my mind like a birthmark. I recall my conversation with the guard on the hill.

You want to make a woman go mad? You take away her baby.

"Why are you here, Abbott?"

"I met Hex at the dockyard. I was doing some work with Emmett when he came looking for a boat. Paid a hefty sum in supplies."

"Did he say why? Did you know he was coming here?"

"Not at first, but then he mentioned the Hill."

Clouds roll in as if ordered to mark the mood. The air cools.

"So you thought, *how convenient, my sister lives there. Let's go abduct her.*"

"I thought I could help you escape when he wasn't looking."

"And you thought I'd just leave everyone behind? You might be my brother, Abbott. We might look alike, but you think nothing like me. I'm not leaving the Hill. Not with them, and not with you."

CHAPTER 29

Sections 5.9 – Do not fear death. Fear things going back to the way they used to be. Before the Colony. Before the Hill.

I HEAD UPHILL. Wind pushes the tears down my cheeks. I wipe away their remnants when I close in on the eating mats. The mood up on the Hill is festive, the scene bustling, as though I've walked in on a hive. Flavored smoke billows from the smoker made from a reclaimed oil drum—a Departed Girl's genius. My mouth waters—a welcome change, even though my heart hurts. Soup simmers in a pot suspended over the cooking fire. The Smalls sit in a semi-circle around one of the Mothers, ripping apart greens. It's the perfect Assignment.

"Where's Quinn?" The lead Collector asks. "We're ready for the Grounding Ceremony."

I scan the crowd of girls and see Quinn draped beneath the arm of another Hunter. Has she already moved on?

"Quinn," the Collector calls over me. "Hurry up, it's time."

I step out of the way as they gather for the Grounding Ceremony. I'll catch up, but for now, I kneel among the Smalls, take a handful of greens, tear them to bits, and add them to the growing hill in the middle of the blanket. Arrow, who was mixing something in a bowl with a wooden spoon that's both too big for the bowl and too big for her hands, stops what she's doing and jumps onto my lap. She overwhelms me with kisses and falls sideways, laughing, her arms wrapped tight around my neck.

I imagine this is what life looked like minutes before I was separated from my mother and put on the boat. *Was I holding onto her for dear life?* A pang of sadness rips through me. I exhale and force a smile.

Arrow touches my patch, as she always does.

"Not too hard," I say, closing my eye as her pointer finger makes contact. She traces the perimeter of the patch repeatedly.

"Your eye hurt?"

I shake my head.

"Then why do you wear that?"

The Mother across from me listens for my response.

I flash back to Abbott's picture and close my eyes. "So my mother wouldn't forget me."

Arrow contorts her lips like she's satisfied but has no idea what I'm talking about.

"Let me take your ponytail out," I say, unwinding a thin rubber band from the knot on top of her head. She winces when the band gets caught, and I have to tug it out. "Sorry." I ruffle her hair. "Doesn't that feel better?"

She jams her thumb in her mouth and nods. She's too old to be sucking her thumb, but I ignore it and pull her into my chest.

"Okay," I say after a silent minute that I wish could last all night. "I have to go."

She slides off my lap obediently and crawls back to her place, where a pile of nuts awaits her small, destructive hands. She takes a rock and begins violently crushing them into bits.

My mouth is dry. I can't find my canteen, and I drag myself to the graveyard in the Westside Forest, parched. Despite its function, it's a lovely place. Many of the trees here are stunted. They have short trunks and long, sweeping branches that form a canopy over the clearing, like protective hands. Wildflowers are scattered over the ground in random clumps, mostly purple ones with robust stems that look like they could grow through metal.

The girls are gathered around the burial hole. Its small size cripples me. Beside the grave is a gray wooden crate that was salvaged from the Hill. The boards on one side have been replaced with a mishmash of scrap wood. When I join their circle, Abena kneels down and places Anouk inside the box, still wrapped in her red blanket, her stuffed rabbit tucked securely under her arm. The Forager opens Anouk's hand and deposits a square of dried plum. The Supplier adds a tiny whittled spoon. Quinn places an arrow next to her, almost the length of her body. The rabbit, I assume, was Anouk's special toy from her Mother, so the last girl to add to the box is a Collector. She reaches into her sack, which is too long for her and hangs down to her knees, and pulls out a small figurine.

"What is it?" My voice comes out louder than I expect. An explosion.

The Collector holds it up into a swath of sunlight that bends through the overhanging trees like a lit path. "It's a boat."

"So it is."

She crouches and sets the boat upright like it might sail around the crate, on the opposite side of the arrow.

"Here's to hoping the way to the afterlife is by water."

I go last. I remove a bead from the Leader necklace and place it on the center of her chest. It shines almost majestically, as if it might have the power to restart her heart.

"Light," Abena says. "She'd like that."

I lean in to whisper into Anouk's ear. It is the tiniest ear. I trace it with my finger, ending at her lobe, which is both soft and cold—which is when I notice something peculiar. Something I've never noticed before.

A hole in her earlobe, like Harlow.

"What?" Quinn sees my hesitation. She hovers over me.

"Nothing." I stroke her earlobe in case the mark is a speck of dirt. I search the other ear for a matching mark, but there's nothing. I sit back on my knees, away from the body.

Pierced lobes, eye patches, a missing fingertip, maimed skin. They are means of identification. The girl with the holes in her ears—Harlow's mother came back for her.

And my brother for me, the girl with the patch on her eye.

Quinn places the lid on the crate, then pulls out a hammer and a handful of nails of varying length. All are rusted. With a few quick blows, the crate is sealed shut. She and the Collector maneuver the box and lower it into the hole. Through the slats, the bead twinkles and then disappears under layers of earth. I stand up and wipe away tears I wasn't aware were falling.

CHAPTER 30

Section 5.2 - By completing your training on the Hill, you will possess all the skills, competencies, and trades necessary to keep the Colony operational.

I LEAD THE exodus out of the graveyard. When we're far enough away that the dead can't hear us, I turn to the girls. "Thank you. I know it's been a tough couple of days." I avoid eye contact with Quinn.

Abena, exhausted, starts crying, her shoulders rising and falling in a jarred dance.

I rest my fingertips on her forearm. "We're taking the night off. The girls need it. Try to have some fun." The Collector looks doubtful. The rest of the Leaders look at me wearily, their bodies drooping with fatigue. "I know it seems inappropriate given what we just did, but the girls need a distraction. And so do we." I take a breath. "Tomorrow we meet after breakfast and talk defense."

"Offense," Quinn says.

"Yes, and offense."

Abena asks, "Shouldn't we have some girls assigned to defense right now?"

The Collector shifts her weight from one foot to the other nervously. "Yeah, I thought you said they were coming back?"

"They are coming back. But they're not coming tonight."

Abena wipes her eyes. "How do you know for sure?"

"A hunch," Quinn says, pointing to the sky as though a picture has emerged on the horizon.

The girls exchange confused looks.

I knock Quinn's pointed finger out of the air. "Emmett's dead, their boat's gone adrift, they have no food, and there's fewer than ten of them. *That's* why they're not attacking tonight. Not because of a hunch." I look at Quinn. "It's logic. Besides, Roman overheard them scheming. He would have said something if they were coming tonight."

Abena still looks concerned.

"And for the record, I have someone on lookout."

Quinn's eyebrows bend, trying to figure out whom.

"Please. Try to relax tonight. We need this as much as the rest of the girls."

The Supplier blows out an exaggerated sigh. "Okay."

We break up. The Leaders head back toward the Quarters, except for Quinn.

I grab her shoulders. "I think I've figured something out."

"What now?"

"Harlow."

"What about her?"

"Do you have any strange markings on you?"

Quinn raises her arms and gestures to her face. "I'm covered in them."

"Not those. Like a scar?"

"You know my body."

"Some of it." I blush.

Quinn avoids eye contact and traces the back of her neck. "Just the ink," she says. "Like you."

"But I also have a patch."

"And long arms."

"Enough with the long arms. I'm being serious here. Harlow had holes in her ears—distinct ones. They were even mentioned in the Record. Abbott said we all have more than one Mother. Like Hill Mothers and Colony Mothers. Real ones."

"Do I have a Colony Mother?"

"I think so."

"What does this have to do with Harlow?"

"I think her Colony Mother sent for her."

"Why?"

"Because maybe she didn't send Harlow here voluntarily. Maybe the Colony forced her to do it. I think she's the one who tipped off the Mainland, exposing the Colony and the Hill."

Quinn releases an exasperated breath. I open my mouth to speak, but notice Abbott standing ten feet away. I make eyes at him, the what-are-you-doing-here kind, and then I take Quinn by the shoulders again and gently shift her body to the left, so she doesn't see him.

"Listen to me," I say. "We're going to figure this out. The truth. It's only a matter of time."

"We don't *have* a lot of time."

"I know, but for now, go find your girls. Gather the Hunters and go be their hero."

I pull her into me and motion aggressively for Abbott to make himself invisible. He gets the message and conceals himself behind a tree.

"Right," she says, turning to leave. "Aren't you coming?"

"In a second," I say. "Have to pee."

She leaves without a fight, and it's me who exhales with relief, like I've just taken a hundred-pound rucksack off my back. When Quinn passes, Abbott steps out from behind the tree. "I didn't mean to interrupt."

"You're supposed to be on lookout."

"I know. I just had a thought. Emmett had a phone with him."

"Yeah. He also had a copy of the Manual on him. You know anything about that?"

"That was mine."

"Why on earth would you have a copy?"

"Our mother."

"Explain, Abbott. I don't have time for incomplete answers right now."

"I was supposed to protect it, in case something happened to the Colony. Something permanent."

"That was a huge fail."

He looks down, offended. "I trusted Emmett. He was a good man. None of those boys would have gone through his stuff. The Manual was supposed to be safe with him."

"I suppose you couldn't have predicted he'd fall off a cliff. Anyway, I have it now. What about the phone?" I hear laughter in the distance, along with a playful shriek, for the first time in days. I walk toward it.

"You know where it is?"

"In my pack, I think. Used it as a flashlight. They're super handy. Why?"

"We might be able to use it to get help."

I shrug, unsure how. "The screen was cracked."

"It should still work. As long as the battery's not dead."

"Who are you going to call?"

"Can I have it?"

I charge through the forest, stepping over toadstools, weaving through ferns. "Follow me."

We go to the Quarters. Abbott waits outside while I search my pack. Quinn's left the hammer she used in the Grounding Ceremony on my mattress.

I return empty-handed. "Can't find it. I think Roman might have taken it back. He seemed to know how it worked."

Abbott kicks the ground. "Darn it."

I shrug. "Sorry. No Manual, no phone. You're on your own."

A group of girls skip, using a long, tattered rope. A few others grapple, tying up and then pushing away. A Supplier removes rust from a hunk of metal with a coiled sponge.

"I hope that's for pleasure," I say. "No Assignments tonight."

"It will be if I get it working," she replies.

I don't know what *it* is. Abbott shakes his head. We continue down, passing the cooking fire. "If you see anything suspicious, come find me. One sharp whistle if it's an emergency. We'll know to arm up."

He pauses as if reviewing the instructions in his head and storing them for future use, and turns to look downhill. The Rock stares back, unmoving.

"The mark behind your ear," I say. "The Colony gave it to you?"

Abbott instinctively traces the *X* on the back of his neck and nods.

"Are you really a servant?" I ask. "To the Colony? The Manual says it's a place only for girls and women."

"It is, mostly."

"Mostly?"

"Boys born into the Colony remain with their Mothers until they turn fifteen. And then . . ."

"You have to leave." I cut him off. "A Departure Ceremony."

"I wouldn't call it a ceremony, but yes."

"And the mark means?"

"Means they won't kill me."

"I can't promise I won't kill you." I wink.

He walks heavy-footed downhill toward his post.

I call after him, "But I will bring you some food."

He flips a lazy thumbs-up without turning around.

CHAPTER 31

Appendix D – Even minute amounts can cause hallucinations, nausea, and euphoria.

AN OBSCENE-SIZED piece of meat is hauled out of the smoker on a spear. It takes two Suppliers to maneuver it to the prep station.

"Double-smoked," one says as they pass by.

"Pheasant," Quinn clarifies.

Lennon emerges from the Quarters with the four-string guitar. I think of the BIG BROTHERS ROCK pin. She has a band around her head to keep her hair off her face. She settles herself onto the same rock she always plays from. When she is situated satisfactorily, she brings the guitar across her body and starts to play.

The song she plays is one she made up about a girl who paints herself into a bird. She adds layers and layers of color to her body, until one day, she looks so much like a bird she turns into one and flies away. Perhaps this is why Arrow thinks we turn into birds when we get to the Mainland.

I laugh to myself as a Supplier hands me an over-flowing plate of food. Pheasant, mushrooms, greens, and a round, sweet-smelling biscuit. My plate, though chipped, has a perimeter of bulbous pink flowers. They are foreign flowers. I try to imagine their scent. We found an entire box of plates and bowls buried beneath a layer of broken furniture once. Miraculously, not a single piece was broken.

The Smalls play a circle game, something someone invented during free time. The girl who's *it* has to close her eyes and make her way to the outside of the circle of girls holding hands. It's pointless, but for whatever reason, it always elicits laughter. It doesn't take much.

Elsewhere, girls chat by the fire. A storyteller keeps a gaggle of Collectors enraptured, her eyes wide and gestures even wider. Girls react with exaggerated expressions. Behind a heap of tools, a Supplier and a Forager kiss, their hands all over each other. I blush and look away. I think of Roman, wishing his hands were all over me, his tongue inside my mouth again. I think of Quinn.

With not so much as a bow, Lennon breaks into another song, her fingers strumming wildly on the four strings. Arrow dances on her toes with biscuits in both hands. Her belly curves outward, full.

Quinn sits with the Hunters. They, too, look full, a few of them sprawled on their backs, limbs relaxed, clenching their stomachs in a good way. Quinn lifts her chin slightly as I pass. I wink. She smiles a half smile. It's reluctant, but real. When this is all over, we'll go to our favorite place on the Hill and cross the ridgeline to the nook in the rock face. We'll go late at night, when the world sleeps and the stars fall, and we'll forget about the Colony. We'll forget about Assignments and rules and manuals. We'll forget about boys. Instead, we will remember us.

At the prep station, I hand my empty plate to one of the girls.

"I need another," I say. "For our lookout."

The girl nods and loads the same pink flower plate with a hoard of meat and mushrooms.

"No greens left," she apologizes.

"All good." It's a generous portion. Before I leave, she hands me a biscuit, which I eat, though it's intended for Abbott.

When I'm halfway down the Hill, I stumble over my canteen. I shout an enthusiastic, "Yes!" into the darkness, like I've found something much more valuable—it's what we call the Collector's rush, a thrill buzz when something useful is uncovered or excavated. I set down his food and take a swig, washing down the remains of Abbott's biscuit before collecting the plate and continuing on. It tastes off. Stale, but it still manages to quench my thirst. Sort of.

The girls' voices get quieter as I move away, but they remain jovial. Optimistic. Stars in a black sky. It is completely dark en route to the Rock, but I could do the trip with both eyes patched, so the blackness doesn't faze me.

What fazes me is the sudden twitching in my muscles. The sensation starts in my calves, as if they're being pinched from the inside out. I stop, nearly dropping the plate, which now feels like the weight of a shield on my left palm. I touch my lower legs, but the twitch moves up my body into my upper legs. Like microscopic crabs are climbing up my ligaments and bones.

The feeling moves through my body. I struggle to hold the plate. I struggle to walk. The path turns into a wavy strip. The Rock begins to separate from the land. The earth pulls away from it and rolls down the hill. I try to scream, but the muscles in my face fail to open my mouth. My face feels like it's melting off my body.

"Wren?" he calls my name somewhere in the darkness. I can't see him. My brother. But my left arm feels lighter now. Maybe he's taken the plate, or maybe I've dropped it. The wavy strip I'm walking bends upward at an impossible incline.

"Wren?" he says again.

I try to answer, but all of my energy goes into taking another step. I feel heavy as an oil drum, a deer hide line-drying in the sun. I hear a crash. I've dropped the plate in front of me.

The flowers around the rim grow into stalks. They burst forth upward into the night clouds while the meat morphs into a four-legged animal and stampedes downhill. The overturned mushrooms whisper my name in a sinister fashion. I try to stomp them to bits, but they reform with each blow and grow bigger.

"What's happening to me?" I say out loud, but I'm unsure if I'm coherent. It feels and sounds like I'm talking underwater.

A light comes on. Manufactured. I feel its heat bouncing off my face.

"Abbott," I say, all lit up like a ghost.

"No, no," the voice says. "Abbott is over there." The light travels to the Rock, which is still there despite the fact I saw it roll away only minutes ago. Abbott is leaned up against it, mouth gagged, his hands behind his back. I suspect they're tied. Across his bare chest, someone has written TRAITOR in a crude black substance. The letters scramble.

RIOTART. ATTORIR. TRA

The light comes back to me. I attempt to smack it out of the way.

"Whoa there, beautiful," the voice says. "You hit me in the face, I'll hit you back ten times harder."

He's lying. I know because it's Rifle Boy. I don't bother to call him out on the fact that he didn't hit me back ten times harder the last time I smoked him. I try to spit on him, but my mouth doesn't cooperate, and I end up spitting all over myself.

"That's attractive," he says.

I wonder if there are others he's talking to in the dark.

"I see you found your canteen." He turns and says, "I can't believe it worked," to someone I cannot see. "On the Mainland, we call this a party drug." He twirls the stem of a leafy stalk. In the other hand, he tosses a spiky seedpod into the air and catches it. The spikes resemble gnashing teeth. They are terrifying.

I recoil, slurping in a line of spit hanging from my

face. I look away from his eyes, which seem to be pulsating. My head spins.

"Don't worry," he assures. "It'll wear off shortly." He removes a square of cloth from his pocket and gently wipes the remaining saliva off my chin. "But until then, why not spend some time getting to know your brother?"

From behind me, someone grabs my arms and binds them at the wrists. I throw up in my mouth. A gag comes next, the cloth gnarly and metallic-tasting.

"Come on, Hex," the boy behind me says. "We don't have a lot of time."

Hex puts the cloth back in his pocket and leans in toward my face. I worry he'll kiss me, but instead he laughs in my ear. It sounds like a thousand people laughing. Then he bites down on my earlobe. I cock my head away, unable to stop the bleeding, and stagger toward my brother.

CHAPTER 32

Section 5.1 – When you defend the Hill, you defend the Colony. You defend humanity.

I WATCH THEM go. There are five, maybe six of them. Eight. I lose them in the shadows. There could be a hundred.

When I reach Abbott, he wrestles to stand, his hands still bound behind his back. He staggers toward me, eyes sympathetic and fixed on my bloody ear. In a few frantic jerks of his shoulder, his upper body twisting, he frees himself. He pulls the gag from his mouth in a downward motion so that it hangs like a kerchief around his neck. I forget that I can barely walk and crumple to the ground, my legs made of straw.

"Is there another way up there?" he asks, dragging me into a seated position. He makes quick work of my knotted wrists. I turn my hands in circles, opening and closing my fingers into fists. "Guess you've never tried jimsonweed."

I shake my head and feel my brain skate back and

forth. A chopping sound cuts through the air, forcing me to plug my ears. At first, I think I'm losing my mind, but Abbott hears it too. He looks into the sky. I can barely lift my chin, but I catch a glimpse of a helicopter tip beneath the clouds, a tall person ducking below a short door. Blue-green lights shine from the tail, which makes the thing look like a metallic whale. "A—a helicopter."

"Yes," Abbott agrees. "Two of them."

"W-what are helicopters doing here?"

Abbott studies the sky while I attempt to stand. "Mainlanders."

"Why are they here? They never come to this side of the island. Never." I stop to catch my breath. My teeth feel like they might dissolve.

He glances upward. "Maybe they'll keep going."

"Look—how low—they're flying." I have to focus on constructing every word.

"Can you move yet?"

I stand, one foot at a time. Abbott looks like he's swaying back and forth, as if one of us is on a boat.

"Take a few steps."

I clunk forward like a piece of metal. It feels like my feet are on backward, but after a few more paces, I find a rhythm.

"Can you go any faster than that?" He fidgets impatiently.

I don't know what he's talking about. I feel like I'm running, but then he imitates me, and if it's even a remote likeness, then I have to move faster. He grabs my arm and pulls me behind him. Arrow used to drag around a one-armed doll. Its eyes blinked open and closed whenever its head bumped the ground. Everyone but Arrow found it creepy.

"I think I'm going to get sick."

Abbott drops my arm and pulls at his hair, exasperated.

"It's not my fault," I say before projectile vomiting. It trickles downhill like I've emptied a bucket, but it makes me feel better. I wipe my face on my sleeve cuff and then reach for him to resume pulling me uphill. He takes my hand reluctantly, unconvinced it's not covered with barf, and we jolt forward.

A third helicopter appears over the Quarters. "There's nowhere to land there," I ramble.

Abbott says, "They don't always need to."

As we approach the Quarters, the helicopters fly in a low circular pattern, a trio of predatory seabirds, their spotlights crisscrossing like limbs engaged in a complicated dance. The wind generated from their propellers sends my hair sideways. Even Abbott's shorter hair whips around recklessly. I think of Harlow emerging from the forest as Finn described, waiting for the helicopter to land, waiting for it to take her away. Her pierced ears, black beacons.

Abbott runs ahead. I lose him in the darkness, only to catch a glimpse of him seconds later in a passing spotlight. He strikes someone in the face and gets clocked in return with punishing consequence. Chaos.

I step on Lennon's guitar, snapped in half, strings bent and the body blood-spattered. I pick up the long end and hold it with two hands, one on top of the other, poised to use it as a weapon. I take a step when I see Quinn fall.

It happens in slow motion. Her cheek vibrates when her face hits the ground, the force of the impact reverberating through her soft tissue. I feel it in mine. I lunge forward, dive on top of her, as the heel of a boot stomps downward into the side of my lower back. I contract my muscles to stave off the pain, as if the harder I tense, the less it will hurt. When I get to my feet, Hex spits in my face.

I take a rogue swing with my left arm. He ducks and uppercuts my chin, causing me to bite my tongue. My mouth fills with blood. From the ground, Quinn traps him by hooking his ankle with her foot. With the second foot, she kicks him in the knee to the ground. He falls, and I jump on top of him, blood flinging out of my mouth. The smell is like I'm bleeding pure iron.

"Get him, Wren," she says. Her voice speaks of exhaustion. I wrap my arm around his neck and spread my body weight over him. Beyond his head, I see the legs of another girl, her feet turned out at an angle the way Emmett's were after he was dead. My body softens with grief, and Hex frees himself, ending up on top of me, full-mount.

He wraps his hands around my neck. I feel my breath disappearing as his thumbs press into the depression above my collarbone. I try to peel his fingers off, and when I fail, I shift to the side, trying to make space between our bodies. It breaks the choke, and I struggle to stand. Out of my periphery, Quinn, too, is trying to get up.

The spotlight finds us. Hex and I instinctively reach up to block the light. Then a ladder swings into view, several feet out of reach. A voice booms, "Grab on." It's impossibly loud. The voice of a mountain. Is this a rescue operation? If so, for who?

I have no intention of grabbing on. The ladder swings away and returns, almost hitting me in the face. The voice again: "Grab on." Familiar. It's Roman.

In the light, I see him, body half-in and half-out of the helicopter, one foot balancing on an upper rung of the ladder, an enormous cone held to his mouth. He begins to descend as Hex goes for my hair. I place my hands on top of his, spin inward to face him, and knee him between the legs. He folds into himself and groans. A chunk of my hair entwined in his knuckles glints gold in the light. He drops sideways to the ground and tucks his knees into his chest.

"Come on," Roman says, placing a thick hand on my shoulder. "Let's go."

I whip around. "I'm not going anywhere."

"Wren," he says, with pleading eyes.

"Take *him*." I point to Hex, still in a curled heap and grunting intermittently. "He's the one that needs to be rescued."

Hex raises his hand in defeat.

"Why, Roman?"

"You asked for my help."

"I told you to help Clover."

"And that's why I called them." He tosses his thumb skyward. "Her arm needs to be amputated. If she doesn't get to the Mainland in the next twenty-four hours, she'll die."

"Where is she?"

"She's already gone," he says. "They promised they'd get her to the hospital."

"And you trust them?"

"Yes, I trust them," he yells. "I saw how hard they tried to save my brother." Tears well in his eyes.

I look up, noting that one of the helicopters has vanished. I cover my ears, avoiding the obnoxious propellers. "That explains one of them, Roman. But why are there two more? Why are they here?"

He shakes his head. A Small screams in the dark. A nauseating pitch.

"Not good enough." I storm away from him, surveying the destruction in front of me. Hex is gone. I turn back to see him climbing the ladder. I pick up a rock and hurl it at him, but it bounces off a rung and tumbles downhill. He's concentrating too hard to react, dragging his body upward. Quinn carries one of the Smalls on her back. Arrow? I run to Lennon, who kneels beside Blue. Through sobs, she breathes into her mouth. Roman blows past me and takes over, striking her in the chest with stiff-armed pumps, the way I tried to save Emmett.

A boy bleeding from the back of the head reaches out his arm. His fingers tremble. He looks young and terrified. His cheeks are gaunt. He's all bone—the face of someone who was hungry before he arrived. I step in, fighting the urge to help him when the remaining helicopter lowers to the ground. We are beside the prep station, the only flat portion of the Hill big enough for one to land. It settles with surprising precision near the body of the blonde from the Mainland. I don't have to get close to her to know she's dead.

The passenger door opens, and a man not unlike Emmett in size and stature steps out. He wears a plaid shirt, his hair long and tangled. He approaches with a heavy jog.

"Let's go," he says, swinging his arm forward, his hand the size of a bear's, fingers trying to pinch my shirtsleeve. "We've been waiting for you."

I take a step back and feel for my knife. It's not in my pocket. "I'm not going anywhere."

The man scoffs and scratches his chin, which is covered in a grotesque pattern of hair. "Tsk, tsk, tsk," he says, his lips cracked and blistered. "That attitude's not going to serve you well on the Mainland."

"Him first," I say.

The man looks down at the poor boy, whose body now rests on his elbows and knees. Blood drips down his forehead. The man cringes. "Come on, boy," he says. "Get in." He gestures toward the helicopter. "You're next, princess." He winks and licks his filthy lips.

"I—I just need to get something."

I rush to the opening of the Quarters and meet the blade of an ax wavering above Abena's head. When she sees it's me, she drops it haphazardly, nearly clipping my shoulder. I exhale with relief. Before I have a chance to ask where Quinn is, she steps into the light.

"You need to get everyone down to the tunnel," I tell her. "The one that leads to the village."

"The tunnel within the tunnel?" It would sound sarcastic if it weren't for the circumstance.

"Yes."

"Are they gone?"

"Some are, but they're trying to force us to leave too."

"Why?"

"It's my fault." Roman stands at the door, eyes downcast.

Quinn's fists clench. "I told you not to trust him."

Roman throws his arms up defensively. "It was an accident. When we couldn't do anything to stop Clover's infection from spreading, I used Emmett's phone to call the hospital. They must have traced it. At first, it was just the one—the medics. They took on her on a backboard and gave her an injection. No sooner did it take off, when another arrived. He put a gun to my head."

"You've got to go *now*, Quinn."

She steps around me, peeks outside, and comes back, hand on her heaving chest. "There's a bloody helicopter *right there*," she says. "How in the heck am I supposed to get by without them seeing?"

"Go out the back."

"It's sealed off."

"Then unseal it. NOW."

The girls in front of me wince but hustle to the

back of the Quarters. I grab Quinn's elbow before she follows.

"Stay in the woods," I say. "Follow the perimeter until you reach the tunnel. You've got to get out of here before they find you."

"What about you? What about the others?"

"I'll take care of Lennon and Blue. We'll meet you in the tunnel."

"When?"

"I don't know." I am desperate. "Just get out of here."

She steps away, but I pull her back and kiss her mouth, quick and tight, so she doesn't even have a chance to react. Just in case it's goodbye. "Go."

I watch until she disappears around the corner. The place has been ransacked. Beds are overturned, hammocks slashed. Personal items strewn over the place, not unlike an open excavation. All that's left of the mirror is the frame and a pile of shards. I turn away from it all and slip back outside.

CHAPTER 33

Section 5.2-1 – At the age of fifteen, your training is complete. A Departure Ceremony will release you back to the Colony.

THE MAN WITH the plaid shirt assists another boy onto the helicopter. The boy can walk, but he drags one of his legs and cradles his left arm. His back is hunched like an invisible foot is stepping on it. When the boy is inside, he bends to pick up a girl. My heart catches. Who is it? He carries her over his shoulder, sets her down near the firepit, and examines her neck with a thick thumb stroke. He's looking for the marking of the Colony, but she's one of them. The other girl with the patchy hair and loose legs. He kicks her in the direction of the helicopter.

Lennon and Blue are still on the ground. Blue partially sits up. In the light, her face looks colorless and sick. Near death.

I sneak over to them. "Get out of here."

"I can't walk," Blue says.

"You have to, or you're next." I point toward the helicopter.

"I'll say no," she says defiantly.

"Doesn't work like that. He'll drag you onboard by your hair."

"Then what do we do?" Lennon asks, desperate. Her shirt has been torn nearly clean off her body.

Roman squats beside me.

"Get them out of here," I say.

He hesitates.

"Get them to the tunnel," I repeat. "You caused this. Do something."

"What about you?"

"I can take care of myself."

He picks Blue up off the ground, and she gasps in pain or surprise, draping her arms loosely around his neck. "Which way?"

"Can you run?"

He nods.

"Then run for it. Past the Rock. All the way."

He repositions Blue in his arms, causing the veins in his upper body to bulge like garden rows. "Hang on," he says.

Lennon looks left and right and takes the lead downhill.

"Stay out of the lights," I shout after them.

It takes me a second to notice the helicopter Roman flew in on is gone. I search the sky and notice a blinking of light before it disappears behind a mob of clouds.

"Hey," the man in plaid yells, "let's go."

I turn to determine if it's me he's addressing and not someone else, but it's only us. A showdown. I ignore the body that's facedown in front of me, a knife jutting from the left shoulder blade. A girl. I try not to focus on the extinguished cooking fire or the mass of charred debris smoldering in the pit. Faint lines of smoke coil upward, unraveling the contents of the fire.

I take a haggard step in the direction of the helicopter, like I've been maimed in battle.

The man smiles and waves me in, his pelvis rocking forward. "Come on, sweetheart," he chides. "Mainlanders don't bite. At least, not hard." He laughs at his joke and moves toward me.

I hold my hand up to stop him, a gesture to indicate that I must do it on my own, as though the achievement is necessary and life-changing. He plays along, stepping back and crossing his hands patiently in front of him.

"I forgot," he says. "You girls can do everything. You don't need help. You don't need boys or men. Look what we did to the earth." He chuckles louder than before. His teeth are brown shells.

There's commotion in the helicopter—people jostling for a seat. He turns his back, distracted. I stop to buy time and think about making a run for it. I doubt he'll give chase, but then a hand beckons from the open door of the helicopter. I step forward to get a better look. Abbott. What does he think? That I'm just going to jump aboard?

He climbs out, says something to the man in plaid, and rushes over.

"Come," he says, breathing heavily. "Please. Come home."

"This *is* home."

"There's nothing left of it!" He makes a sweeping gesture with his arm. "I'll get you to our mother."

A swirl of wind, as if commanded by nature herself, lifts debris from the fire into the air, almost encircling us. Bits of paper. A palm-sized piece flitters down into my open hand like a petal. The hand-written script on the surface is from the Record. A few words remain, a crude yellow-brown line indicating the fire's last bite. I fold my hand around the paper and dash back inside the Quarters. The trunk carrying the Record and The Manual is upside down. Fragments of paper decorate the floor like broken tiles. Abbott arrives at the entryway. I hear his heavy breathing before he says anything.

"I'll never go to the Mainland," I say through barely audible, clenched teeth. My fingers bend like metal under force into closed fists. I open my mouth to say it again, but a nauseating wave floods my body, and I have an immobilizing flashback. My mother. The one from the picture that Abbott showed me. My mom clutching a pillow, the same print as my patch. Or maybe it's not a flashback, and it's just a made-up memory. I reach out to touch it.

"Let's go," Abbott says quietly, as if he knows I just experienced a moment greater than birth or flight or death.

I move forward in a trance-like state, stepping on bits of the Manual as if my mother and I are magnets being drawn together across hills and ocean and time. I want to see her. I get closer to Abbott, who stands at the entryway but repeatedly looks back in the direction of the helicopter.

"Come on," he urges. "He's coming."

I snap back into reality. The frantic state of the situation returns, and my heart sprints, adrenaline kicking in like a strong dose of medicine. A drug. Jimsonweed.

"I can't just leave." I shake my head. "Come back for me."

"It's not that easy, Wren."

I kneel down and start gathering all the paper, what's left of one of the books. I don't stop until I've collected every piece.

"Bye, Abbott," I say, walking away. Brother.

I round the corner to the rear, and I hear him tell the pilot. "She's gone." I don't wait to listen to any more of their conversation. I reach the unsealed rear exit, now a gaping hole of dust and rock, and step through, hugging the paper, our identity, the Hill.

CHAPTER 34

Section 5.2-2 – Upon your return to the Colony, a new Assignment will be bestowed upon you.

FROM THE WOODS, I watch the helicopter lift off the ground. It wobbles like a poorly manipulated puppet, but after a certain height, it dips sharply to the left and makes a sweeping turn with the grace of an eagle. A spotlight passes at the edge of the woods once and then a second time before it goes away. I don't move. I wait in the darkness for the sound to dissipate, and when it does, I step onto the open face of the Hill.

What everyone else saw as bleak and pathetic now seems so. The parts of the Hill under excavation look like open wounds, like the split-open stomach of a dead seabird. Plastic tops where there should be organs. Junk where there should be dirt. Bodies. Still, there is beauty in the girl-made grid that divides the Hill into boxes. The stakes are perfectly measured, the ropes taut and well-knotted, the reclaimed sections covered with grass and hope.

I tuck the remains of the Record and the Manual under my arm and bend to pick up a flower that's been stepped on. I peel back the translucent petals, which are splayed against the ground, and pull it free. The blossom is too heavy and dangles like a head held in shame. I cup it and secure the stem between my fingers, bringing it to my nose. It smells sad.

When I reach the Rock, I place the flower back on the ground, a rehabilitated animal being released back into the wild. I find a flashlight that looks like Roman's, except it's yellow plastic and only the size of my hand. I flick it on, and it emits a bright, almost-blue light. I stick it in my pocket without turning it off and attempt to run up the side of the imposing stone, handicapped on one side, where the papers are still clutched under my armpit. My body is drained, and I'm forced to get a running start. Three times before I'm successful. On top, it feels five degrees colder, and I stand rigid like a fortress to keep it from penetrating my lightweight clothing. Over the side, I see Abbott's discarded gag. I wonder what he will tell our mother. In the emptiness, part of me wishes I went with him. I picture what life would be like on the Mainland with a mother and brother, but it's like imagining life on a star.

I sit down and turn my back to the beach, to the wind, and pull the salvaged papers from under my arm. I shine the flashlight on the first page—a piece from the Record detailing Clover's arrival and Assignment. The next three pages are also profiles: Blue, Harlow, Arrow. I shuffle them to the bottom of the stack and continue.

There are bits from the Manual: ASSIGNMENT GUIDE-LINES, DEPARTURE PROTOCOLS, NAME-CHOOSING CER-EMONY PROCEDURES. All of the pages are torn, many outlined with patterned bootprints, spotted with blood. Scattered in between are random notes: *How to Identify Toxic Materials, Edible Plants and Animals. Killing and Preparing Fowl, Constructing a Bow and Arrow.* Another profile. I want to rip it all to shreds.

Where is the stuff about the Mainland? Where is the section on what to do after an attack? Where is the truth? I roll the stack of papers into a tube and shove it in my pocket. I need to get to the tunnel.

I slide part way down the Rock and jump the rest of the way down. My knees weaken on impact. I tread downhill toward the opening, my body almost numb. The opening has been left gaping, a screaming mouth. Not that it matters. No one's around. I prepare to enter feet-first when I hear something from the beach. The disjointed inhales of someone crying.

A girl.

How difficult was it to stay in a group? I step back onto the path and down to the shore.

A boat lies perpendicular to the water. One of ours.

There shouldn't be.

The crying escalates from inside the shallow fishing cave on the far side of the beach. I recognize her immediately.

"Nova? What are you doing here?" I want to run to her and away from her. Is she alone?

She jumps to her feet.

"Wren," she says, yanking my shirt, her eyes drifting, wild. "It's horrible there."

"The Colony?"

"The Mainland. We never made it to the Colony." She looks like she hasn't slept or eaten in a week.

I think back to the Departure, how Nova was one of the few girls actually excited to go, and then I flash back to the image of me cocooned in a blanket, my face the size of a moth. "But there's mothers there."

"Mothers? Is that what you think?"

"*My* mother's there."

"So is your Assignment."

I stare at her suspiciously. "You know my Assignment? On the Mainland?"

"Yes," she says, "though I don't know his exact name."

His name? "What's that supposed to be mean?"

"The only Assignments on the Mainland are men."

The water chops and spits at our feet. My thoughts do the same. "We have to go. The girls are waiting in the tunnel." Nova looks confused. She doesn't know about the tunnels. "It's a long story. Just follow me."

"The men found about the Colony."

I charge forward. "We've heard, but what exactly does that mean, Nova? What's actually happening over there?" It's like having a conversation with Roman or Abbott or the dead guard or the man in plaid.

"We were almost to the Mainland. We could see it— shells of buildings lining the shore, all rebar, and open windows—but before we could dock, they surrounded us."

I stop in my tracks. "Who?"

"Men."

"And then what?"

"They transferred us to another boat, a rusted-out cargo ship painted red that smelled of oil. There was a circle of men. And that's when the auction started."

"Auction?"

"Girls sold to the highest bidder."

"You escaped."

"I jumped." She looks over her shoulder nervously, like there's a possibility she's been followed.

"Don't worry," I try to assure her. "They've already come and gone." I carry on upward, the walk getting easier as the path transitions from sand to solid ground.

"No." She grabs my elbow roughly and yanks me backward.

I spin to face her, seething. "Didn't you see the helicopters?"

She shakes her head and her already-enlarged eyes continue to expand, like they've been chemically injected. Her lips are so chapped, they barely resemble lips.

"By ship," she says. "They're rounding up everyone from the outlying territories."

"For what reason?"

"To defeat the Colony. The men on the Mainland are preparing for battle. They need numbers. Soldiers, mercenaries, sacrifices. They've been combing the waters, abducting anyone who can help them fight." Tears fill her eyes. In the moonlight, they look like marbles, the kind you find sewed into stuffed animals.

"How do you know this, Nova?"

"There was an announcement the day I escaped. Then I saw them depart. The same men who intercepted us. They're organized. They're angry."

We reach the mouth of the tunnel. Nova looks uphill. Traces of smoke, the remains of spot fires, mark the dark sky like gray ink. The quiet is haunting.

"What—what happened here?"

"Boys," I reply. "Boys happened here." I sit down with my feet dangling inside the hole, preparing to lower myself inside. I motion for Nova to crouch beside me and muscle my way down, my heels skidding over the loose soil.

She follows behind and nearly kicks me in the back.

At the bottom of the entrance slide, I pull out the yellow flashlight and light up Nova's disturbed, gaunt face.

"What is this place?"

"There's a complete tunnel system under here," I explain. "I think it used to be a mine."

"For what?"

"Don't know." I take her hand and pull her in the direction of the alternate tunnel, recalling Roman's instructions. "Over here." I climb up the pile of rocks resembling the cave-in and find the opening. It's smaller than I imagined, and I gulp with discomfort.

"You've got to be kidding me," Nova says, her feet plunking down heavily in the small space beside me.

"You jumped from a cargo ship and survived." I get down on my hands and knees. "I'll go first."

CHAPTER 35

Section 8.4 – Do not be fooled. There are no good men. It is not in their nature.

THE HEIGHT OF the tunnel remains low for a good twenty paces, but eventually expands, so we can get off our knees and move in a semi-upright position. It smells like earth and lost time, a place you'd expect to find skeletons and the remains of things extinct. Nova coughs nearly in rhythm with each step, grating my nerves.

When the ceiling opens up well above our heads, we both stop and instinctively stretch, grabbing our lower backs in tandem.

"That's better," she mutters.

I agree and twist side-to-side in an effort to further ease my spine. I brush debris from my knees and keep going.

"How much longer?" Nova asks, waving something away from her face.

"There should be a few rooms off to the side." I don't

tell her I'm wondering the same thing. The eerie silence confuses me. I figured we'd at least hear the uncontrolled murmurings of the Smalls by now—Arrow, who can hardly contain herself, who was banished from naptime at two because she could not settle. She should be bouncing off these walls.

"It's awfully quiet," she comments, her shoulder brushing against mine as the tunnel curves left like a tail.

I ignore her observation and tread faster. We move in silence for several minutes, passing beneath a series of gray wooden struts fixed to the ceiling, their rusted nails, the size of mushroom caps, protruding at various depths. I shiver.

"Stop," Nova says, driving me to a halt. "A door."

I spin the flashlight in the direction of her gesturing hand.

"A door? For a rabbit, maybe." I crouch down and run the blue light along the perimeter of the arched doorway.

"Go through," Nova says, giving me a slight shove.

I duck and enter sideways. The doorway is a foot thick and opens into a small room. The ceiling is high, relative to the space's width. Other than us, it's empty.

"Where are the girls?" Nova asks.

"I don't know," I snap. "Stop asking questions." She's starting to remind me of Quinn, who I suddenly wish was here with me, finishing what we started. I miss her. "There are other rooms." I hunch back down and exit through the tiny doorway. Anxiety quickens my pace. I adjust my patch, which feels damp and irritating against my cheekbone.

Twenty feet later, another room. A much bigger door. Nova breathes heavily as she half-jogs to keep up. The room is empty.

I wave the flashlight around shoddily, looking for signs of occupation, but it's as if we're the first ones to cross under the doorway in a hundred years. I crash into Nova as she attempts to enter and I try to leave. She frowns and holds her shoulder where we made contact.

She opens her mouth to speak when we both hear footsteps. I flick off the flashlight. An image of her alarmed face remains in front of me like an apparition, and then disappears into the blackness. I feel her nudge by me into the room. I freeze, my back pressed up against the wall beside the doorway. I hold my breath for as long as I can and exhale in small, indistinguishable spurts.

Who's coming?

The footsteps get louder, flogging the tunnel floor with purpose. I contemplate slipping through the door to join Nova, out of view, but a faint glow swells in the distance. The blurred circle of a flashlight. Roman, I think as the body bears down the tunnel. I hear his breath, a slight wheeze as he closes in. When I'm certain it's him, I call his name. "Roman?"

He skids to a messy stop, as though he'd been running on ice and was about to hit a dead end. He clutches his heart, like he might be able to coax it out of his throat.

"Wren," he says, bending over, bracing himself on his knees.

"Where are they?"

He stands up, his chest still visibly rising and falling as he tries to regulate his breath. "Our village."

"I told you to wait for me here."

Nova cautiously emerges from the adjacent room. We both pause to look at her, but we continue without me offering an introduction.

"That's why I came back," he says. "They wanted to go all the way to the village."

"They?"

"Well, Quinn, anyway."

"Quinn made that decision?"

He looks at me with weary eyes. "The Smalls were crying, Blue was bleeding. She insisted we go there for help."

A rush of pride warms me like a pair of hands on cold cheeks. Suddenly, I can't wait to be reunited with Quinn.

"Village?" Nova leans on me for stability, her body trembling against mine.

"My village," Roman qualifies. He reaches down and takes my hand. I hold it for a moment, reveling in the power of the gesture. Part unity, part relief, and part desperation to be pulled the rest of the way by someone physically bigger, stronger. But I let go. A searing pain shoots through my head, like lightning penetrating my skull. I stagger forward, nearly collapsing into Roman, who steadies me up against the wall.

"Wren?" Nova asks, her voice troubled.

"Wren?" Roman echoes. "What is it?"

"Are you sure they made it?" I flick on the flashlight with hands that don't feel like mine and head in the direction of the village.

Roman picks up his flashlight and follows. "Of course I'm sure. I took them as far as the last room, and they continued on from there."

I stop. "But how do you know they made it?"

"There's only one way out." He throws up his hands. "They had less than a hundred meters to go when I turned back to find you."

"I have a bad feeling."

"I told you they were coming," Nova says.

We both stare at her for a moment and then run.

CHAPTER 36

Section 5.7-1 – The Head Girl accepts abso-
lute responsibility for the Hill during her
tenure.

THE TUNNEL FEELS infinite in length. Just when it feels
like we should be hitting the end, the space narrows or
turns sharply, reducing our pace. Nova lags behind and
hollers for us to wait, which we do for long enough for
her to catch up before we resume our frantic pace. After
a slight decline, Roman stops and I smash into him, not
paying attention.

"This is where I left them." He ducks into the adjacent room, vacant and dank.

Nova uses the break to catch her breath and ease a
side stitch. She sounds like she's going to cough out her
organs. "I need water."

"Soon," Roman says, moving forward.

We run at a pitiful pace through the remainder of
the tunnel. Blood soils the back of Roman's arm, but
he doesn't seem to notice. He slows to a walk, and
Nova and I follow. The mouth of the tunnel is wide but

difficult to access as the ground curves up at a steep incline, like a ramp. Roman pulls himself through first, then reaches down to drag me up behind him. Poised on the edge of the opening, we work to bring Nova through together. She's deadweight; it's like pulling up an anchor. I fall backward when her upper body collapses aboveground, the trees bending overhead. My flashlight spins and sets something ablaze, a speck. I crawl toward the tiny light.

"What is it?" Nova asks, brushing debris from her chest.

I pinch the jewel between my fingers. "It's from Arrow's necklace."

Roman doesn't wait. He plows through the brush, making a beeline for a clearing that is blanketed by clouds of black smoke, thick and aromatic. I struggle to keep up, covering my face with my sleeve. With my flashlight fixed to his heels in the distance, I stumble and fall face-first on a network of exposed tree roots. A piece of skin dangles from my chin. I press the flap back into the wound.

Nova whimpers behind me. I can tell by the sound effects she's moving in a zigzag pattern, her voice bouncing from my left ear to my right and back again to the left.

When I reach the village, Roman lets out an awful, animalistic cry, like he might transform into something mythical and deadly. I stay in the shadows, behind the ruins of what I presume was a house.

Flames pounce on the remaining structures. Blackened timbers litter the land like grave markers. Nova catches up and waits with me in silence. The only thing left standing is the village flagpole. Roman kicks it savagely with his heel, the way one might try to kick down a tree. For a brief second, a wind blows through, causing the village flag to flap. It hangs by a thread.

I rub smoke from my eye as I watch Roman fall to his knees, his hands in fists, his forehead balancing on the ground. I move in to comfort him, but before I can crouch down, he starts beating the ground with his fist, yelling inaudible things from the dark places inside him.

Then I see her.

Him.

Draco limps out of the smoke and into the firelight. His fur is singed, eyes sad and aware that something is wrong. Everything is wrong. His resolve flounders.

"Roman," I whisper. "Look."

Roman draws back onto his heels. Draco hobbles forward, yelping with each step. Roman can't get up fast enough. He scrambles to his feet, his center of gravity skewed, heart trampled. "Draco," he says, collapsing into the dog a few feet away.

I step back, distracted by what appears to be a watchtower on the opposite side of the settlement. I tiptoe away, leaving Roman to process his reunion with Draco and the guilt of what's happened here.

"Nova," I call out. "See what you can do for the dog. She—he's special."

The watchtower resembles a tree house without a roof. Its construction looks shoddy, but when I shake the ladder, which stretches high into a black opening above, it barely wavers. I jam the flashlight inside my shirt and climb hastily, anxious to see what the view might reveal.

When I reach the top, I pull myself through the opening, my body relying on my triceps to guide me through. Once on deck, I retrieve the flashlight, which has fallen and rests at my belly button, out of my shirt. Nothing but trees in front me. I nearly gallop to the left, and it's more of the same. Rows of conifers, their fat cones nestled in the high branches like nests, bend in the wind. I pass to the other side and shine the light. An abyss. Nothing.

Then, out of nowhere, a ship of unconscionable size moves into view, towering out of the sea like a piece of fiction. A tall tale. It's exactly what Nova said was coming.

It's now leaving.

"Roman!" I scream, my hair whipping in my face. I wait for a response, annoyed my breath is so heavy that it's all I can hear. I scream his name again, high-pitched to the point it actually fades out. This time, I cover my mouth, breathe into my cupped hands and try desperately to listen for him.

But I hear a different voice behind me. "Wren?" It is weak and small, like it's coming from a speck or from inside my own head. I once again consider the possibility that I'm going crazy, that I'm hearing evidence of my own trauma, but it happens again.

"Wren?"

I spin around and pan the flashlight through the space.

It lands on Arrow, curled fox-like in the corner, her sallow cheek resting upon tiny clasped hands. The flashlight falls out of my hand and rolls toward her.

"Arrow." My voice sounds distorted, barely able to speak, as if her name came out of the spaces between my teeth. I bend down and touch the back of her arm, which is cold like Anouk's always was. "Arrow," I say again. She lifts her head off the ground and she shifts into a seated position and reaches.

"Pick me up," she says, her voice just above a whisper.

I grab hold of her waist, and she latches on, securing her ankles and wrists behind my back and my neck. I hold her head and cry into her hair. Behind me, Roman emerges from the ladder. His eyes are red, and he staggers into the watchtower, exhausted, as though he's climbed through a cloud. "Look." Still clutching Arrow, I point to the ominous dark ship beyond the shallow curve of the island's north shore.

Defeated, he places his hands on the rail bolted to the tower's perimeter. The wood is withered gray and carved up. I imagine those assigned to keep watch up here, the loneliness of the midnight shift, the bitter cold of winter. Roman stares out at the ocean, ink-black and unwieldy, tracing a marking with his finger. I maneuver the flashlight over his hand, his shattered knuckles.

He pulls away, exposing her name: Tora.

I say it out loud, the fire crackling in the background, fifty feet below.

"My mother," he replies, dropping his head.

I place a hand across his slumped shoulders. "Your mother," I whisper. "She came here."

"She fell in love."

Love.

Arrow presses her cheek into mine. Backlit by climbing flames and dangling wire, Nova binds Draco's paw. Somewhere out there, Quinn's devising a plan—the oldest, not left behind, but *taken* away. The new Head Girl.

"Now what?" Roman asks. He is defeated, flat, hopeless.

I take his hand.

"Now we go the Mainland," I say. I sound defiant, like Quinn. "We go to the Mainland and we bring them back."

ACKNOWLEDGMENTS

FOR THE GIRLS who shirk the rules and shake the earth and shun the plans others made for her.

To my immediate family—my husband Dave and children, Pippa, Hugo, and Odessa, the great entertainers, teachers, and champions in my life, who infuse their love, energy, and wildness into my heart, my head, my work, and our home.

To my writer friends, my lifelines in craft and companionship, Leanne Shirtliffe and Brad Somer. I love you muchly.

To my rabbit, Alfie, for reminding me that love is gentle.

To the indomitable women who worked on this book: my agent Stacey Kondla, my cover artist Eglė Plytnikaitė, my editor Larissa Melo Pienkowski, book designer Frances Ross, and my publisher Jennifer Baumgardner.

To my mom, my go-to for all things writerly, humanly, spiritually. My dad and Reta for their steadfast encouragement and whole support. To my sisters, Amy and Amanda, for the beautiful mess that is sisterhood. I love being your baby sister.

The Biancas, Jennies, and Judiths in my life, who bring me joy and wisdom and laughter and know-how.

And to all the women who've influenced or touched my life, whether through their actions—*especially their actions*—their advocacy, and their art: I am grateful. I am a better me because of you. It is a very long list that includes rappers, mothers, caregivers, strangers, sculptors, rescuers, fixers, leaders, little ones, fighters, rebels, workers, bus drivers, volunteers, researchers, and writers.

"Be not afraid, only believe." Mark 5:36